IAN PARKINSON was born in 1978 and studied philosophy at the University of Central Lancashire before working as a civil servant and insurance clerk. *The Beginning of the End* is his first novel.

THE BEGINNING OF THE END

THE BEGINNING
OF THE END

Ian Parkinson

CROMER

PUBLISHED BY SALT
12 Norwich Road, Cromer, Norfolk NR27 0AX United Kingdom

Printed in Great Britain by Clays Ltd, St Ives plc

Typeset in Sabon 10/13

ISBN 978 1 78463 026 3 paperback

1 3 5 7 9 8 6 4 2

THE BEGINNING OF THE END

PART ONE

I

I ALWAYS WONDERED whether I was going to find the body of a young woman while I was out walking the dog. That's how they're found every other week on the evening news – by men walking their dogs. I liked the thought of visiting the corpse after work to see how things were progressing. I didn't see why you had to go and immediately call the police. Besides, it would have given me something to do.

I'm not particularly fond of dogs. I'd certainly never wanted to own one – or any kind of pet for that matter. A homosexual living in the apartment at the end of the corridor asked me to look after the thing shortly before committing suicide. There had been a knock at my door. I didn't answer. I never answer the door. It was usually a representative from an electricity company wanting to know if I was happy with my current electricity supplier. They would be going from door to door. But I'd disconnected the doorbell years ago. Usually they pressed it once and left me alone.

I was sitting in the dark watching television. I muted the volume and whoever it was knocked again for what seemed like a minute. Even if they'd heard the sound of the television they had no right to knock for a second time like that. I thought about opening the door and going along with everything they said, and at the last minute, when I was just about to sign whatever piece of paper they pushed in front of me, I'd say that I'd changed my mind and close the door in their face.

I turned the television off and sat in complete darkness in case they could see the light from the screen. But they knocked again even louder than before. It sounded as though they weren't going to stop until they got an answer. I made no effort to disguise my irritation when I finally opened the door.

'I'm sorry to bother you. I live a few doors down . . .'

I didn't say anything. The dog was standing next to him on a leash; a small thing with a ridiculous haircut.

'I was wondering . . . I've asked everybody that I know . . . My friends, people in the office. I was wondering if you would be able to look after my dog? I know it's really rude of me to ask, but I have to go to the hospital to visit my mother and I won't be back until tomorrow night.'

I didn't know what to say. If he'd been a representative from an electricity company I wouldn't have had a problem saying no and closing the door. He was in his sixties and I could tell from the histrionic tone of his voice that he was homosexual. He'd been crying, too – his eyes were red and swollen. I had no reason to doubt the validity of his story.

'His name's Vincent,' the man said. 'I'll go and get his things. A tin of food a day and a little walk before bedtime and he's fine. That's all he needs. He's the happiest little dog in the world. But if you want to spoil him he likes buttered toast for breakfast and a play with one of his toys after his dinner. Don't you . . . ?'

The man knelt down beside the dog and stroked its head. When the dog rolled on to its back, he burst into tears. I tried my best to ignore him. It was probably a performance to make it difficult for me to refuse to look after the thing. But the homosexual still hadn't returned for the dog two weeks later. I called the police to tell them what had happened, but they didn't seem interested. The telephone operator told me that the police had more important things to worry about. Besides, it wasn't a crime to leave a dog with someone. When I asked to file a missing person report the operator got irritated and suggested that I should make an attempt to solve personal disputes myself.

Eventually they sent someone to investigate and a body was found in the man's apartment. His name was Thierry and he'd slit his wrists and electrocuted himself with a radio in a bath of water.

2

I'VE NEVER SEEN a dead body. I was over thirty years old before I went to a funeral for the first time – a disabled colleague who had been suffering from some sort of disease. We worked in different parts of the building and I'd never spoken to him.

My grandmother died when I was thirteen, but I didn't go to her funeral. I was allowed a day off school and I stayed at home and played computer games. Thierry's funeral was held on a Friday afternoon and the crematorium was over forty minutes away. I thought about taking the dog, but the traffic would have been horrendous and it wouldn't have been an appropriate place to ask his family what they wanted to do with the thing, whether I should get rid of it myself.

I'd been hoping to bump into a relative in the corridor outside his apartment. A specialist cleaning company had been contracted to remove any signs of putrefaction from the bathroom. Occasionally someone in white overalls and a mask would carry a black bin bag out to the lift. I stood and watched on my way home from work. A neighbour opened her door and began a conversation with me. The death had given everyone along the corridor something to talk about.

'It's terrible,' the woman said. 'I'd noticed the flies and the smell.'

'Who's in charge of the removals?' I asked.

'I'm not sure. As far as I know it's the local authorities.'

'He asked me to look after his dog on the night he killed himself. I've been wondering what to do with it.'

'Did you know him then?'

'No. I'd never spoken to him before.'

'Poor thing. I bet he's wondering where his owner is.'

I nodded my head. The dog had been barking constantly during the day when I was out. There had probably been complaints made against me.

'He's been barking during the day,' I said. 'Have you heard anything?'

The woman thought for a second. 'No. I don't think so. Which apartment do you live in?'

'Forty-seven.'

The woman looked along the corridor to my door. 'I'm not sure. I'm not usually back from work until nine or ten. Do you live on your own?'

'Yes.'

'At least it'll keep you company at night.'

I nodded my head in agreement. But I didn't really agree with her. You had to pick up its faeces when you took it for a walk, otherwise you were liable to be prosecuted. Almost every lamp post in Leuven had a sign on it to warn you. I'd never really noticed them before. I'd had to buy some special plastic bags and a scoop. The only good thing was that some of the women on the internet sites I subscribed to said that they liked dogs, especially taking them for long walks in the countryside. I'd taken some pictures of him with my mobile phone and uploaded them on to my profile page on PARTNERS.COM.

I'd been using internet sex sites for years without much success. I'd learnt to write that I enjoyed healthy outdoor pursuits like mountain biking and rock climbing, as well as the more obvious things like going to restaurants and the cinema.

But nothing seemed to help much. I wouldn't say that I was particularly attractive. I have a thin, expressionless face and a small chin that seems to want to hide inside the loose pocket of skin hanging underneath it. Sometimes I think that my appearance has a vaguely sinister element to it.

3

I'D BEEN WORKING at Siemens for nearly fifteen years. It was a job like any other. I sat at a desk for seven hours and twenty-four minutes a day. No one seemed to know why, exactly, it was seven hours and twenty-four minutes. The twenty-four minutes in particular were a mystery.

During the fourteen years and eleven months that I had worked at Siemens I had never once been promoted, even though I'd applied for a promotion on three separate occasions. To apply a fourth time would have been ridiculous. I told myself that my third rejection would be my last. It would have been less humiliating if they'd asked me one evening as I was leaving simply never to return to the building.

When I graduated from the École Nationale Supérieure des Arts Décoratifs I was as optimistic as any of the other Industrial Design students. Optimism comes with the territory. You will never find a pessimist amongst the design fraternity. But optimism had followed socialism and Christianity into my personal oblivion, all of them leaving my body one after the other like tired rats queuing to abandon a sinking ship.

Of course I never envisaged myself employed designing doorbells and washing machines. It was not an ambition of mine. Like every other design student I was convinced that I was going to be the next Dieter Rams or Mies Van der Rohe. Ron Arad and Philippe Starck were to be my contemporaries.

I would become their friends and we would go from party to party in Paris and London. I would soon make them jealous of my brilliant new way of seeing the world and dealing with its everyday problems, but only in a friendly, amicable kind of way that wouldn't spoil our mutual respect for one another.

My third application for promotion had been rejected seven years earlier. I slowly realised that I was engaged in the struggle of the survival of the fittest. Our nondescript concrete building on the outskirts of Leuven was an environment much the same as a jungle in central Africa. The same struggle was being waged in every sector of commerce and industry – in art and literature, in law and politics, in supermarket retail and professional sports. So many millions of insects scrambling over one another at the bottom of an enormous bucket which, sooner or later, will be emptied into a toilet bowl and flushed from memory.

Like every thirty-something, I gradually gave up, so slowly that I didn't really notice an incremental abandoning of all my former beliefs and ambitions. Naturally, I threw away my expensive leather biker jacket and my canvas shoes, ceased making my weekly visits to an expensive hairdressers' in Brussels for a beard trim. Male designers have a habit of dressing as though they're in a boy band. It isn't a good look for men that are generally in their forties and fifties by the time they are famous enough to have their photographs taken. Female designers dress like New York bohemians. On the whole they role up the sleeves of their T-shirts and you're left with the impression that they don't shave their legs or armpits. But I don't know. It was difficult for me to see things clearly.

4

BELGIUM HAD BEEN voted the most boring country in the world. Everybody was talking about it. It was on the news every night for a week.

In fact, the news channels were a constant disappointment. Every evening I hoped for a passenger jet to have crashed into a city, preferably something worse, something unimaginably terrible, only to find the newsreaders talking about something that didn't interest me in the slightest. Once or twice a year a celebrity would die unexpectedly.

I turned the television on and muted the volume. A reporter was standing on a street in front of a large building somewhere in Brussels. I looked at the time in the corner of the screen. In two minutes there would be a weather update. Sometimes they had a blonde-haired woman I liked doing the weather reports. I sat on the couch and looked at the dog. It no longer bothered to move from its basket when I returned to the apartment. For a few weeks it had made something of an effort to greet me when I got out of bed in the morning and when I returned home from work in the evening, but now it rarely seemed capable of such affection. I didn't like to touch it and it had clearly sensed a general antipathy on my part. I got the impression that it was suffering from depression. Occasionally I would stroke it with one finger.

After a car advertisement there was an advertisement for a moisturising lotion. When the weather report came on the blonde-haired woman smiled and gave a brief summary of the weather so far today as she walked in front of a large screen displaying a satellite image of the earth. She was wearing a knee-length black skirt, high-heels, and a colourful blouse. Her breasts looked larger than they usually did, probably because of the blouse. Maybe she was wearing a different type of bra. As she turned towards the screen, raising her left arm and flattening the palm of her hand over the contours of a coming depression, I pictured myself lifting her skirt and parting the cheeks of her backside.

The microwave bleeped in the kitchen. I didn't know which meal-for-one I'd chosen because I hadn't bothered to look at the picture on the front of the box. I didn't have a preference. I wasn't surprised to find that it was a curry. I ate it sitting on the couch in front of the TV while I watched an old episode of The Vampire Diaries. When I'd finished I flicked through the music channels to see if there were any new videos I hadn't seen.

I turned the news off when I was eating. Usually they didn't show anything they considered too upsetting: maybe a blood-stained street, or the half destroyed facade of a building spattered with pieces of arms and legs. The slightest thing would make me lose my appetite. Insects were even worse than dead bodies or exploded human body parts. I found it almost impossible to watch a wildlife documentary. A swarm of ants seething over a dead rat had once made me vomit.

In short, I was something of an hysterical neurotic like everybody else. I couldn't touch raw meat without heaving. I ate nothing but processed food from plastic cartons. I never touched the door handles in public toilets and I still found it necessary to wash my hands perhaps forty or fifty times a day. For the purposes of total sterilisation, I kept a small bottle of alcohol gel in my desk drawer and in my car's glove compartment.

At nine in the evening, after perhaps ten or fifteen minutes of prevarication, I reluctantly turned the television off and put on my jacket. The dog climbed out of his basket and followed me to where his lead was hanging on the coat rack, his tail swinging slowly from side to side, his head raised in anticipation. I'd tried letting him out to defecate on the balcony, but it was less than three feet wide and after two hours he'd barely managed to urinate.

I stood at the door and looked along the corridor to see if I could hear anyone. Again, I considered whether to carry the dog to the elevator so that none of the other residents could hear his overgrown claws on the polished linoleum. But again I decided not to bother. Perhaps a letter of warning would force me to make the effort to get rid of the animal.

Outside, the night sky had cleared and the air had turned cold. I hunched my shoulders to hide my face from the security cameras, and made my way across the car park to an unlit footpath where the dog could defecate in the darkness created by several trees, and where it wouldn't be necessary for me to pick up its warm faeces. By the time I'd walked the short distance to the end of the path and back, my patience had run out. It was clear that the dog wasn't going to do anything, either out of protest or because I hadn't remembered to feed him. Tomorrow I would have to lock him out on the balcony when I went to work, in case he shat in the living room.

I dragged the dog back to the elevator, again hunching my shoulders and lowering my face so that I wasn't identified by the security cameras. The corridors were empty and silent. It was possible to believe that the entire building was unoccupied. I'd lived in my apartment for three years, and until the homosexual's body had been found, I hadn't spoken a single word to any of my neighbours. Before that I'd lived in another apartment in a different part of Leuven. Once or twice a month, the old woman next door would ask me to open her tins of soup. Sometimes there would be thirty tins of soup, and as I stood in her kitchen opening tin after tin until my hands and wrists were beginning to ache, she would use the opportunity to talk to me about the news or the weather. In the end I decided to buy her an electrical tin opener. After that she didn't find the opportunity to speak to me much.

5

AGNES HAD BEEN working at Siemens for five years. I liked to watch her walk from her desk to the printer, or from her desk to the coffee machine. Each day she wore something different, perhaps even something new that she'd bought the evening before on her way home from the office. I can't remember ever seeing her wearing the same item of clothing on consecutive days. If one day she wore the pink stockings and short grey skirt combination that I liked, I knew that she wouldn't be wearing them again for at least two or three weeks. I found consolation in the fact that she'd probably buy something even more interesting to look at.

On Thursday evenings she went to a Thai boxing class. She hated exercise but she wanted to lose weight. And besides, there was a man at the class she liked. He once offered to take her home in his sports car and she accepted even though her own car was parked in the gym car park. I overheard her confiding the story to a female colleague. I'd already come to the conclusion that I had absolutely no chance with Agnes myself. She was young and beautiful, and I was in my thirties and divorced.

Occasionally I would email her to see how things were going. She always replied within a few minutes. I found the speed of her replies quite encouraging. Sometimes we would discuss one of our colleagues and I would try to ask her if there was anyone in the office that she liked. I could see her desk from where I was sitting, but her face was often obscured by her computer screen, so it was hard to know what she was thinking.

I thought about following her home after work. Maybe she would stop at a supermarket and I could pretend that the whole thing was a coincidence. I'd been thinking about it for a while. I needed to confront her, but I didn't want to do it in the office in front of everyone. Whenever I'd tried to ask for her mobile phone number she'd always changed the subject. I knew that she was probably trying to tell me something, but I needed to be certain about things.

There was a rumour that she'd been having an affair with my manager for the last six months. It seemed fairly typical, but they'd certainly kept it well hidden – you would never have thought that there was anything going on. As far as you could tell, their relationship was strictly professional. Nevertheless, my manager was in the process of divorcing his wife.

Agnes knew perfectly well what she was doing. Fucking the boss certainly wouldn't do her any harm. Besides, the manager was relatively wealthy. The thought of that alone was probably enough. The whole thing made me depressed. I'd been considering making more of an effort, buying some new shirts and trying harder with my colleagues. Perhaps I would have been able to get a promotion.

I confided everything to Bernard, one of the IT assistants responsible for the computer system in our building. We'd met in a health and safety training group. Very occasionally we would organise an evening out. He suggested I go to Thailand. He told me that internet sex sites were a waste of time. In five years he'd still only managed to get three or four fucks out of them. Most of the women were bored housewives who just wanted some attention – dirty emails and pictures of cocks to cheer themselves up.

'I go to Thailand every year,' he said. 'I fucking love it. You can do anything. Whatever you want. Twins, sisters, mothers and daughters – everything. And it's not like they hate you. Most of them want to marry you, even if it's just to get a settlement visa.'

It was certainly worth considering. I'd lived alone for longer than I cared to remember. On Saturday afternoons I would buy a porn DVD. Once or twice a month I would go to a massage parlour.

6

I STAYED IN bed for over a week, watching television and masturbating almost continuously. When I was hungry, I would order a takeaway on the internet. Taking a frozen meal-for-one from the freezer and carrying it to the microwave would have required too much of an effort.

After two days I'd run out of alcohol. I ordered some bottles of wine and a case of beer from the supermarket. Thankfully the delivery driver was uncommunicative. He barely looked at me as I collected the shopping bags from him. I'd been worried that he would want to talk to me about the weather or something.

I'd been watching one of the shopping channels all afternoon. I climbed back into bed with a bottle of beer as the presenter was demonstrating a new total surface cleaning gel. In the corner of the screen it said there were only 53 complete bottle and applicator systems left for sale.

When I returned to work my manager invited me into his office to complete a back to work report. He told me that he was there to help, that his number one priority was the happiness and general well-being of his colleagues. If there were any concerns, he needed to hear about them. I didn't know what to say. I nodded my head to reassure him. My medication had been increased, but I wasn't in the most stable of mental conditions. I didn't speak unless I was spoken to. Everyone knew to leave me alone.

'If you're suffering, Raymond, I want to help.' My manager frowned sympathetically from behind his rimless glasses. 'We've been telephoning you every day. I even came and knocked on your door.'

I looked at the floor. 'The intercom isn't working properly.'

'You could have been dead. We were close to calling the police. Technically, we should have done. We have certain legal responsibilities to think about.'

My manager uncrossed his legs, and then crossed them again almost immediately. He'd come to join me on the chairs arranged at ninety degrees around a coffee table in the corner of his office.

'Perhaps a few sessions with a counsellor would be a good idea. You don't have to struggle with things on your own. What do you think?'

I hesitated and looked back at the floor. 'I don't know. I've been to see my doctor. I was thinking of maybe going on holiday for a few weeks.'

'That's entirely up to you.' My manager stood and walked over to his desk for his electronic cigarette. 'But think about what I've said. Our company takes its responsibilities very seriously.'

I left my manager's office and walked back to my desk. Francoise glanced at me from the desk opposite. I hadn't spoken to her all morning. Or anyone else for that matter. No one had bothered to ask where I'd been for the past week.

I'd still been married to Anthea the first time I counted the number of words I spoke in a day. We'd agreed to separate and neither of us had anywhere to go, so we had no choice but to sleep in the same bed. Hardly a single word would pass between us from the first thing in the morning to the last thing at night. Three or four nights a week I would sleep on the couch. It was uncomfortable and I would wake up in the early hours of the morning with a terrible backache. Sometimes I would be sitting at my desk at five or six a.m. I started to speak only when I was spoken to. It was difficult to go an entire day without being forced to reply to a direct question, but I would always try to make my answers brief – one word answers if possible: yes, no, probably. I soon realised that it was perfectly acceptable to ignore your colleagues.

7

THE DOG HAD been doing well since I'd started to take him to an obedience class. The class was held every Tuesday evening on the playground of a local high school. Most of the other dog-owners were grey-haired women in their late fifties and early sixties, but the dog behaviourist that ran the class often recruited the help of a teenage daughter who wore tight tracksuit bottoms and small T-shirts without a bra.

The daughter's name was Anita. I found it almost impossible to ignore her as she jogged up and down the playground with her little spaniel. On rainy evenings, when I didn't feel like taking part in the class, I would sit in my car and watch. I liked to imagine Anita lying on her bed, her face buried in her pillows as I pulled down her jogging bottoms to reveal her little buttocks. I'd even come up with a plan to get her back to my apartment. I would say that I'd been asked to work late on Fridays and that I needed a regular babysitter for Vincent. It sounded like the script for a porn film, but I didn't see why it wouldn't work. I would probably just have to get her a little drunk.

At the end of every class the dog behaviourist often talked about the dog's 'wild nature', or the dog's 'animal nature', or the dog's 'wolf behaviour'. She would gather us around and tell us to sit on the ground, like nursery children being read a story before an afternoon nap. She said that we could learn a lot from dogs. We could learn to be happy.

If it wasn't for her daughter, I would have stopped going to the dog obedience classes altogether. But I suppose they gave me something to do. I was learning something new, and it was good to have the chance to make new friends. Numerous studies have shown that volunteering in group activities outside of the workplace significantly increases a person's longevity and overall wellbeing. Nevertheless, I was bored with the whole thing. Owning a dog hadn't helped me on any of the internet dating sites.

At what I'd decided would be my last dog obedience class, I found the courage to ask Anita if she'd like to mind Vincent on Friday evenings. I called her name from the edge of the playground and she walked over to me with her little spaniel.

'I was wondering if you'd like to look after Vincent this weekend?' I said. I'd never spoken to her before and my voice sounded a little nervous. I could feel my heart beating in my chest.

'I have to work late on Friday and I don't really want him to be on his own. I haven't had him for very long. His owner died and I promised I'd look after him. I don't mind paying you.'

'I'd love to look after him.' She knelt down and stroked Vincent's head, scratching his ears with both hands.

'I was thinking maybe 50 euros would be enough? I'll drop you off at home when I get back.'

'50 euros?' Her eyes lit up.

'If you'd like, you could stay the night.'

She hesitated. 'I don't know . . . I'll have to ask my mum.'

I smiled and watched as Anita walked across the playground to where her mother was setting out a line of orange cones. They talked for less than a minute, occasionally glancing in my direction. Finally, the girl's mother shook her head and Anita shrugged her shoulders and walked away.

'My mum says I could look after him at our house...?'

It was pointless persisting. I should never have mentioned the idea of her spending the night at my apartment. I should have taken my time. I tried to smile, but it was impossible. I walked back to my car and drove home before the class had even started.

8

IN THE END I was given a formal written warning for an unauthorised absence. My manager told me that he'd tried his best, but that there was nothing he could do about it. If I wanted to appeal, I could.

On my way home from the disciplinary meeting I stopped at the massage parlour. Thirty minutes with a girl cost the price of a porn DVD. Four girls were sent into my room one by one as I sat on the edge of the bed. I chose number three – the only one to walk in half-naked. She'd only just finished with another customer. Her cheeks were flushed and a few strands of hair were clinging to the sheen of sweat on her forehead. When she came back a few minutes later she was wearing a bra. She walked around the side of the bed and waited for me to lie down so that she could put a condom on me.

'Do you want me to suck you?'

'Yeah.'

I lay against the pillows as she knelt on the mattress and rolled a condom over my penis, sliding my hand between her thighs, smoothing her panties over her vagina and anus. A large, dark freckle marked the pale skin of her left buttock. I pulled down her panties and pushed the tip of my finger between her labia.

'What's your name?'

'Hannah. Do you want me to go on top of you?' She lifted herself on to her knees and turned to me for an answer.

'Yeah.'

Before leaving the car I'd finished nearly half a bottle of whisky. My breath probably smelt of alcohol, but at least I would be able to hold off from ejaculating for a while. I didn't want to go back to my apartment, but I didn't seem to have much of a choice. If I went for a drive I risked being stopped by the police and breathalysed. I could always go to the supermarket. At least it would give me something to do. Perhaps I could remember the necessary ingredients for the artichoke soup I'd seen being made on a cooking programme earlier in the week. I usually looked in the electrical aisles, too. I'd been considering buying a new microwave.

9

WITHIN THIRTY SECONDS of leaving the runway I was the only passenger not already watching TV or listening to music. I looked through the window at the fields and canals as the plane banked left and continued to climb. A silver car was travelling along a road lined with trees. It was hard to imagine there was a driver behind the wheel. It looked like a metallic blood cell passing along a winding green capillary.

The airline's complimentary magazine had an article about a hot air balloon race across the Sahara desert. I looked at the photographs taken as the sun rose over the dunes on to a valley of brightly coloured hot air balloons lifting into the sky. The text was typical of such publications: "Dawn in the Sahara. And the most beautiful sight I have ever seen appears like a dream as I peer out of my Bedouin tent."

The passenger sitting next to me was watching a film on his laptop and flicking through a copy of *The Rough Guide To Thailand*. Both he and his boyfriend had shaved heads and perfectly trimmed stubble. They could have been twins. I glanced at the computer screen and at a picture in the guide book of some wind chimes taken at somewhere called Chatuchak Market.

When the drinks trolley came I bought a bottle of whisky to wash down two sleeping tablets and put in the ear plugs I'd bought at the airport bookshop. Muffled pieces of conversation drifted below the hiss of the cabin. On the seats in front, someone was practising Thai words from a phrasebook.

'Makeua . . . Aubergine. Makeua Tet . . . Tomato. Plaa Meuk . . . Squid. Plaa Duk . . . Catfish.'

I thought about the homosexual who had left me his dog shortly before killing himself. I'd taken the dog to a dog charity on my way to the airport. I suppose it would have been the last thing the homosexual would have wanted, but there was nothing I could do about it. My apartment was too small for anything larger than a goldfish or canary. The woman behind the reception desk had been obnoxious. I'd had to queue and explain that I'd been left with a dog and that I wasn't in a position to look after it. She shook her head and asked me to fill in a form.

'And you're absolutely sure you can't look after the dog yourself?'

'Yes.'

'But you have to understand that it's extremely difficult for us to find homes for them. Have you considered asking your friends or family?'

'I don't have any friends or family.'

The woman shook her head again. 'I don't have the time to go in circles. As long as you realise how difficult it'll be for us to find a home for your dog. There's a good chance he'll be put to sleep.'

I didn't know what to say. She probably said the same thing to everyone. I started to repeat the story about the homosexual but the woman behind the reception desk leant forward and took the form from me.

10

I WOKE UP at three o'clock in the afternoon. My room didn't have much of a view, but at least it had a balcony. I took a cold bottle of something called Beer Thai from the mini-bar and washed down two tablets.

The woman I'd met on THAILOVELINKS.COM had sent a text message to say that she wouldn't be able to see me until the following afternoon. I sat on the edge of the bed and turned the television on. A cowboy was walking towards an empty building in the desert, his hand hovering over his gun. The image was blurred. His face was purple and yellow.

After I'd finished my bottle of Beer Thai I had a shower and put on my shorts. A couple I recognised from the airport mini-bus were talking to the receptionist as I walked out of the lift. They looked as though they'd been up for hours exploring the city. The receptionist was drawing something for them on a map.

I left the hotel and wandered along the beach road. The heat was terrible. The street signs were the same as in Belgium. Eventually, I managed to find a supermarket. I bought some plastic tubs of cooked noodles and some cigarettes and a bottle of the rice whisky I'd read about in my guide book.

As I passed by a brightly painted burger bar on my way back to the hotel, a waitress stepped from a table of tourists to offer me a laminated menu. Fading photographs of naked Thai girls adorned a price list of sex shows and alcohol offered by the bar. In one, a Thai girl lay on her back on a table, her head between her knees and her arms wrapped around her ankles. What I presumed to be an American with spiked ginger hair smiled broadly at the camera, his teeth exposed in a grimace as he lowered his face to the girl's raised buttocks.

He was deformed, an amputee, the withered stumps of his arms gesturing awkwardly as he posed for the photograph. Given his physique, I guessed that he'd been a US Marine, injured by a roadside bomb in Iraq or Afghanistan and taken to Thailand by his friends as a show of support. Smiling at his undiminished vitality, I realised that the young American wasn't deformed and that he'd inserted one hand up to the wrist in the girl's vagina, and the other up to the wrist in her anus. The ginger-haired man's girlfriend was standing on the other side of the Thai girl's splayed legs, two thumbs up to the camera as an identical grimace of pleasure bared her buck-teeth.

I handed the menu back to the Thai woman and shook my head.

'You want see man fuck sister?'

'Maybe later.'

'Brother and sister. They look same.'

'Maybe later. I need something to eat.'

'You eat and watch show. Hungarian casserole.' She held the menu back out to me.

'I don't really have the appetite for Hungarian casserole.'

The woman turned indifferently and walked back to the table of tourists. The sun was already skirting the tops of the high-rise buildings. Most of the other hotel guests would be gathering on the beach to watch the sunset. On the sidewalk in front of me, a pale German held hands with a small Thai woman as they strolled back to their hotel, their beach towels folded under their arms. They walked in silence, the German keenly watching the traffic as it crawled to the lights up ahead. Occasionally he would mumble at a minor driving infringement, raising his chin and squinting at the mopeds as they weaved between cars.

Back in my room, I drank some of the rice whisky and another bottle of Beer Thai as I lay on the bed and listened to the whirring sound of the air-conditioning unit. I'd been thinking about going out to lie by the pool, but it was nice just to lie on the bed with the balcony doors open and to look at the rectangle of blue sky. I refilled my cup with rice whisky and flicked through the TV channels. A Los Angeles detective dressed in an Armani suit was having a shoot-out with a criminal in an empty warehouse. A loud burst of machine gun fire echoed around the hotel room. On a home improvement programme with a German narrator, a young couple were renovating a dilapidated farm house in Italy. It seemed as though the local builders weren't up to expectations and the couple were getting a little exasperated with the whole situation.

I turned the TV off and put on my shorts and flip-flops and went down to the bar. Two Australian girls were sitting in bikinis drinking cocktails, their blonde hair bleached almost white by the sun. I ordered a bottle of Beer Thai and thought about saying something to the girls, but in the end I didn't bother. They picked up their glasses and walked over to a group of friends who looked as though they'd walked off the set of a pop video. One of them had an afro and another was wearing a pair of enormous headphones.

I lit a cigarette and tried not to look at the girls. I'd been divorced from Anthea for three years, and now I was going to marry someone that I'd met on the internet. Anthea found the fact that she'd only been married for eighteen months particularly embarrassing. But I'd always hoped that we'd eventually get divorced, even if I'd not expected it to happen so soon after our wedding. I hadn't really wanted to get married to her. I suppose it had seemed better than nothing. We met in a nightclub and when we went back to her apartment she licked my anus. If nothing else, at least I had one fond memory of her. Our wedding day had been unremarkable. I remember a baby crying almost constantly in the small registry office, the child of one of Anthea's relatives. Later on there was a disco and I sat with my mother at a table by the edge of the dance floor. She asked where my father was and I said that I hadn't bothered to invite him.

I wandered over to the pool and looked for a sun lounger. Most of them were unoccupied. A couple on the other side were lying parallel to the edge of the pool, following the path of the sun. A tall, overweight German was lying in the corner reading the autobiography of a footballer. I chose a point equidistant between the two and made myself comfortable. I didn't bother to take off my T-shirt. I had no intention of trying to get a suntan.

Joy was probably still with a customer. Perhaps he'd paid for an extra night and she hadn't been able to refuse. It made no difference to me. The wedding ceremony was being taken care of by the marriage agency. I closed my eyes and listened to the sound of the traffic in the distance. After a few minutes I could already feel the sun beginning to burn my face.

The German had put down his book and walked to the side of the pool, readying himself before diving into the water. He was a surprisingly good swimmer, his arms arching rhythmically into the air as he glided the length of the pool. It was inevitable that he was going to try and start a conversation with me. He'd clearly come on holiday alone and was looking to make friends with someone. When I went back to the bar he came and sat at the next table, his shorts still dripping with water. Our proximity made it almost impossible for me to ignore him. I thought about getting up and sitting somewhere else.

'I love swimming,' the German said. 'I used to be on the swimming team at school, but I'm not so good any more.'

I smiled and sipped my drink.

'Have you come on holiday by yourself?' he asked.

'Yes. But I'm getting married in a few days.'

'In Thailand?'

'I'm marrying a Thai woman,' I said. 'We met on the internet.'

'Oh. I didn't understand for a moment.'

I lit a cigarette and finished my glass of beer. I felt like taking another couple of tablets. I couldn't remember how many I'd taken before I left my room.

'I've considered paying for a Thai girl myself, even if only for the company in the evenings. It's my first time on holiday alone. I've been divorced for five years. Usually I go on vacation with my daughter. But maybe I should do what you're doing. My sister did the same thing. She married a black guy from the Dominican Republic.'

The German smiled to himself and raised his bottle to his lips, watching as the beer drained into his mouth.

'It's ridiculous. Every Sunday when I take Claudia back, her mother and I sit about waiting for her to go up to her room, and then we fuck in the garage with the door locked.' His smile faded, his eyes staring blindly at the table in front of him. He was a big man, with the torso of a walrus, and I had the impression that he was capable of sudden bouts of violence. I was relieved when he picked up his book and towel and said that he was going to go and read on his balcony.

'I might see you later . . .'

I nodded and watched him leave. The wet hairs on the backs of his large shoulders protruded from beneath his sports vest. Maybe things would be better for him if he went to a waxing parlour once a month. I'd read in a magazine that a hairy back is probably the biggest turn-off for a woman.

JOY WAS ALREADY sitting at a table outside the Coconut Bar on Beach Road. She looked different to the photographs she'd uploaded on to her profile page, perhaps even more beautiful than I'd been expecting. I hesitated, before walking over and introducing myself.

'I know who you are, Raymond.' She laughed and stood up to kiss me on the cheek. 'You don't need to tell me your name.'

'I bought this for you.' I reached inside my jacket pocket and took out a bracelet that I'd bought at the airport gift shop. 'I thought you might like it.'

'You didn't have to buy me a present, Raymond.' She held the bracelet up against the palm of her hand, turning the jewelled flowers between her fingers. 'It's beautiful. Thank you.'

'Do you like it?'

'Yes. It's really beautiful. What are the flowers made of?'

'I don't know.'

Joy fastened the bracelet around her wrist, smoothing the tip of her thumb against the pattern of flowers. 'So what have you been doing while you've been in Thailand?'

'Nothing. I've pretty much stayed in my hotel room and watched TV. I lay by the pool this afternoon.'

'I went to the marriage agency today,' Joy said. 'I've arranged for the ceremony in the temple garden.'

'What's happening with the settlement visa?'

'We need a marriage certificate first. We can discuss things when we go to the marriage agency.'

I nodded my head and smiled. Joy looked down again at her bracelet, turning her wrist in the streetlight.

'I was thinking maybe we could go for something to eat?' Joy said. 'I'm really hungry.'

'Yeah, me too.'

'Let's go for a walk.'

We turned off the beach road and wandered through the crowded back streets. I could smell her shampoo and makeup beneath the smell of her perfume, and the moisturiser she'd used after she'd taken a shower. The smell of her body reminded me of the bedroom I'd shared with Anthea, the dressing table piled with cans of hairspray and bottles of perfume. I hadn't really smelled those kinds of things since my marriage. Occasionally, a female colleague would brush past me in the corridor or at the printer, and I would smell her perfume and perhaps her makeup mixed with the smell of the washing detergent she'd used to wash her clothes. The women in the massage parlours I'd visited smelled only of the anti-bacterial wipes they used to clean their hands and vaginas.

We found a table at one of the burger bars and ordered some noodles and two glasses of rice whisky. A bored young Thai woman was pole-dancing on a small stage inside. Ignoring the dance music blaring from the speakers above her head, she could barely be bothered to move her body and writhed slowly around the metal pole, gyrating her hips while she watched the television behind the bar.

'I feel like celebrating,' Joy said. 'Maybe we should get drunk?'

'What do you want to celebrate?'

'Meeting you for the first time! We're getting married in a few days, Raymond. Aren't you excited?'

'Of course.'

We finished our drinks and ordered two more whiskies as our noodles arrived. None of the customers were paying any attention to the pole dancer. Every now and again one of the men sitting drinking alone would look up with the same blank expression they had when they looked at the muted television screen.

As we made our way back to the beach road, Joy asked whether my friend Bernard was looking after Vincent. She'd liked the photographs of him that I'd uploaded on to my profile page on THAILOVELINKS.COM. They were probably the reason she'd responded to my friend request.

'I had to take him to a charity. There was nothing else I could do.'

'Are you going to go for him when you get home?'

'I won't be able to. They'll have found him a new home by then.'

'Maybe they won't. You can ring and ask if he's still there.'

'But he isn't my dog. I'm not allowed to have a dog in my apartment.'

'I wanted to take him for walks with you, Raymond. I hope his new owners are nice to him.'

I changed the subject and suggested we go for a walk by the sea. We walked in silence on the warm sand, the waves crashing against the rise of the beach in front of us. After a few minutes, I reached out and held Joy's hand. I could feel my heart beating in my chest. Her fingers felt warm and soft.

'Joy's a nice name,' I said, my voice almost lost beneath the sound of the waves.

'Thank you.'

'Did you choose it for Thai Love Links?'

'No. It's my real name. Lots of girls are called Joy in Thailand.'

Further along the beach, two crows were pecking at the contents of a plastic bag, their black wings dissolving into the night sky as they took to the air above the flashing lights of the bars and discos.

'We should go to Miami Disco,' Joy said pointing across the curve of the beach to a large, brightly lit building. 'It's one of the new big super-clubs being built by the Russians. My friend works there.'

Except for the sex shows, Miami Disco was like any other nightclub I'd been to. We sat on a sofa in a corner and watched the tourists wandering around with their young Thai girls. I'd been considering paying for a night with one of the girls myself. In the end, I would probably have found it easier to go to a massage parlour. When you paid for the girlfriend experience, they expected to be taken to restaurants and to go on boat trips.

In an opposite corner of the club, a group of twenty or so middle-aged Western women was clustered around cordoned-off tables laden with empty bottles. One of the women was wearing a mini-skirt wedding dress and veil, evidently in celebration of her forthcoming marriage. Snaking between the women, a muscular African dancer gyrated his heavy crotch in each of their faces. When it came to the turn of the bride-to-be, the dancer ripped off his thong to a chorus of screams and playfully rubbed his erect penis against the woman's face, ignoring her half-hearted protests. Buoyed on by her friends' shouts, the woman took the dancer's penis into her mouth, jerking her head backwards and forwards before forcing his glans to the back of her throat.

'It seems odd that the stripper's an African,' I said turning to Joy.

'White women don't really like Thai men so much. He's probably American or something.'

Three of the women gathered on their knees around the stripper, wrapping their hands around his muscular thighs as they nuzzled at his testicles and took it in turns to suck his penis.

'Those women are really worshiping that guy's cock.'

'Yeah. White women behave just like men.'

'How often do you get hired by groups?'

'All the time. Men want to be like porn stars when they come to Thailand.'

I liked the thought of seeing Joy getting fucked by five or six cocks. She'd written on her profile page that she wanted to be a porn star and that she'd already been in an American low-budget porn film shot on the island of Phuket in southern Thailand. I'd tried to find the film on the internet, but Joy hadn't even seen it herself and she didn't know what the DVD was called.

We left the club at six o'clock in the morning. I could already feel myself getting an erection as we neared the hotel. Joy rubbed my crotch in the elevator, and as soon as we were inside my room she knelt down and unfastened my trousers, pulling out my cock and tenderly taking my glans into her mouth, her fingers gently massaging my scrotum as I thrust my cock deep into her throat and ejaculated.

I'd forgotten how nice it felt to be caressed by such a willing tongue. I would probably have fallen asleep without sleeping tablets, but Joy had turned the television on and the sound of her flicking through the channels kept me awake. I propped myself against the pillows, watching as she undressed down to her orange G-string and wiped the faded mascara and smeared lipstick from her face before climbing into bed beside me.

I kissed her and slid my hand between her legs and into her panties, her labia parting beneath the tips of my fingers as I stroked her clitoris and looked at her light brown skin and her black hair falling across the pillow. I asked her about the porn film, about how much she loved fucking three men at the same time, how much she'd loved their big cocks. I could already feel myself getting hard again. I wet my glans and moved between her thighs, pushing my erect penis into her vagina.

The early morning sun was shining through the window and a rectangle of light fell across the bed, illuminating Joy's right breast as the silicone implant rocked back and forth over the corrugations of her ribcage. I was in a sunny hotel room with a beautiful young woman and I was about to ejaculate for the second time in an hour. Two days earlier I'd been masturbating in the rain in Belgium. The world was suddenly a wonderful place.

12

I SPENT ALL of the next day lying by the pool. Most of the guests were middle-aged men who had paid to spend their holiday in the company of a Thai girl. They ambled through the chilled hotel reception, pinkly balding and over-weight in their shorts and T-shirts, sweaty-palmed uncles trailing the hand of an exotic niece. As long as they were willing to pay a small fee the hotel seemed fine with the arrangement.

Joy had gone to see a friend before going to the marriage agency and I'd decided to stay at the hotel. She'd said that I didn't really need to go along if I didn't want to.

I flicked through my copy of *The Beach* that I'd bought at the airport. The last thing I could remember was the secret island being discovered by a group of Americans. The char-acter played by Leonardo DiCaprio in the film version of the book was sitting on the top of a cliff with a pair of binoculars, watching some people paddling towards the island on a raft. Or maybe they were swimming towards the island. I couldn't remember.

I looked at the front cover again, at the picture of Leonardo DiCaprio, before finally giving up to go and look for some-thing amongst the small library of books left by hotel guests. Inevitably, there wasn't much to choose from: spy thrillers and various novels of erotic romance in several European languages. I picked out a self-help book called *Discover Your Potential* and flicked through the pages.

Certain words were underlined. Belief. Structure. Fear of Failure. Adaption. Destiny.

When I returned to my sun lounger I realised that the German I'd spoken to was sitting at a table drinking a cup of coffee. He had a small red rucksack with him, stuffed with a beach towel and a bottle of water. I pretended not to have seen him. I didn't want to say hello, let alone engage in a conversation. But he'd already seen me and his mouth was open ready to say something.

'Did you get married yet?'

I looked up and continued to pretend that I hadn't seen him sitting a few metres away.

'No, not yet.'

'I saw you with her yesterday. She's very beautiful.'

'Thank you.'

I was expecting him to say something else, but instead he just nodded with his mouth still open. When he'd finished his cup of coffee he came over and stood by the edge of my sun lounger, his hands gripping the straps of his rucksack and his hairy knees almost touching my arm.

'I was thinking of going to a marriage agency myself. I looked on the internet. But I don't know. I leave in a few days. Maybe I can come back. There's Russia as well, you know. They have the same thing.'

I nodded my head in agreement. I had to admit, a high proportion of the women I'd seen on Russian marriage agency websites were extremely attractive. But for some reason I didn't like the thought of paying to marry a woman who came from a cold country. Perhaps it was because I would probably have to visit her family once or twice a year.

'So when do you get married?' the German asked.

'Saturday.'

'And then your wife can fly to Belgium with you?'

'No. She has to apply for a settlement visa.'

'How long will you have to wait?'

'I don't know.'

'I think it might be better with a Russian agency. That's what I'm thinking.'

He looked across the empty sun loungers at a young girl sitting on her own at one of the tables in front of the bar.

'OK... I'm going to the beach. Saturday's my last day. I'm going home on Sunday.'

I nodded my head. I didn't know what to say.

Perhaps he'd wanted me to invite him to the marriage ceremony. But it seemed pointless, even if it would have given him something to do on the last day of his holiday. It was just a case of signing a few forms. I was hoping the whole thing would be over within less than a few minutes.

Eventually, the German wandered away, disappearing behind the palm trees and a concrete wall topped with a border of pink flowers. The way he walked seemed vaguely sad, stoically smiling at strangers as he passed by them, his pink thumbs tucked into the straps of his rucksack.

I flicked through *Discover Your Potential* and stared at the words *What is the secret of success?*

13

SOMEONE KNOCKING AT the door woke me. It took a conscious effort to remember that I was staying in a hotel in Thailand. The room was dark and a breeze was blowing from the open balcony.

'It's me, Raymond.'

I sat on the edge of the bed and pictured Joy's face. The whole thing seemed like a dream. I must have taken too many sleeping tablets. After a few minutes I managed to walk over to the door, but I couldn't remember how to unlock it. I had to feel the wall for the light switch and look at how the locking mechanism worked. For some reason it seemed like a complicated puzzle, though there were only two movable parts. After two or three attempts with the four or so combinations available, the door seemed to open by itself. Joy walked into the room, dropping her handbag on the bed before picking up the remote control and turning the television on.

'Everything's arranged for us to get married on Saturday.'

I lay back down on the bed and closed my eyes. Joy walked over to the balcony door. I could hear her high heels against the tiled floor and the chafing of her skirt against her thighs. The smell of her perfume drifted over the bed.

I remembered that my mobile phone had vibrated while I was sleeping, a dull and unpleasant sound that had broken through the surface of a dream. I reached across to the bedside cabinet and picked it up. It was from a number that I didn't know. I pressed the 'read' button. The message said that my father had died and that the funeral was probably next week.

The text message was from my mother. She must have contacted Siemens and asked them for my number. Usually the human resources department would have refused a request for personal information, but perhaps they had acquiesced. It seemed reasonable in the circumstances. I couldn't think how else she could have got it. I'd long since stopped bothering to forward my new number to her whenever I changed mobile phone contracts.

'What is it?' Joy asked. 'Is it something important?'

I'd been staring at the screen for a few minutes. 'Not really. It's a text from my mother to say that my father's died.'

Joy didn't know what to say. I shook my head and said that it was nothing, that I hadn't spoken to him for years. I lit a cigarette and stepped out on to the balcony. Joy came and sat on one of the metal chairs.

'We can cancel the wedding, Raymond, if you need to go home. I'm sure they'll give you your money back.'

'We don't need to cancel the wedding. I don't care if I miss the funeral.'

I took a long drag on my cigarette and thought about changing the subject. I hadn't spoken to my mother for years either. It seemed strange that she'd gone to such an effort to contact me. Perhaps she wanted to be the first to give me the bad news. But I had nothing to say about my father.

'My mother and father divorced when I was young,' I said. 'I didn't really see him much after that.'

By the time I went in from the balcony, Joy was asleep in bed. I thought about waking her to ask if she'd like to watch a porn film with me. I felt like watching something with a redhead in it. A thin redhead with pale skin. But she'd had a long day arranging the wedding ceremony.

I climbed into bed with my tablet and typed the words 'redhead' and 'pale skin' into the search box on one of my favourite websites. It didn't take long to find exactly what I was looking for: a young redhead with a large tattoo across her back that really brought out the paleness of her skin.

There didn't appear to be much of a narrative. The redhead was standing in front of a white leather sofa in the middle of a large, sparsely furnished modern apartment. A man in a shiny grey suit walked into the room and sat on the leather sofa, pulling the woman towards him and raising her skirt. As the redhead bent over, the man in the suit spat on her anus and watched the saliva dribble over her vagina.

The sound of the young woman's moans woke Joy. She rolled on to her side beneath the covers, her eyes flickering with the screen's reflection as the man in the suit smeared the tip of his penis around the redhead's anus.

'Look at her ass,' Joy said, her voice quiet and sleepy. 'It's so beautiful. As soon as I have the money, I want to get my ass bleached. I think it's really important.'

I unfastened my shorts and took out my penis, wetting my glans with spit as I watched the movie. The redhead clearly loved fucking big cocks. Joy glanced down as I ejaculated heavily across the sheets, before reaching for the remote control and turning on the television.

There had been a terrorist attack and the moment of the explosion had been captured on several cameras and mobile phones. The sound of a wailing woman reminded me of the young redhead in the porn video. It was ridiculous to scream like that.

I4

Iinspected Joy's breasts on the morning of our wedding day. She'd been standing on the balcony smoking a cigarette and I'd been watching her through the window. When she came back into the room and lay on the bed, I slipped my hand beneath her T-shirt, my fingertips playing over her nipples. I hadn't really asked her about her breast implants. The darkened skin of the small crescent scars was barely noticeable.

'Before I came to Thailand I was thinking about having a penis extension,' I said, raising her T-shirt and smoothing the tips of my fingers over the scar arching beneath her left breast.

'Do you like fucking men with big cocks?' I asked.

'Yes. Do you like fucking girls with big tits?'

'Yes. I like big tits.'

'I want to make mine a little bigger. Not too much. You have to be careful not to go too far. Plastic surgery is addictive. I've had my lips and my eyes done, too.'

'I hadn't really noticed.'

'That's the whole point. It's supposed to enhance your features. Most people get it totally fucked up. You have to know where to go to get something that looks natural.'

'Lots of men like fake breasts. They prefer that to normal sometimes.'

Beneath the warmth of her perfume and deodorant, a faint smell of stale sweat rose from Joy's armpits. For some reason it seemed an odd combination: her body odour clashed with the sight of her large fake breasts. Perhaps she needed to take a shower. For some reason she'd spent all morning at the marriage agency again. I hadn't really shown any interest in the organisation of things. I was pleased to see that things were progressing, but the details didn't seem too important.

I'd never bothered to verify Joy's age. In my guide book it said that thousands of Thai girls work in the sex industry under the legal age limit for consensual sex, some sold by their parents to the owners of massage parlours. On a website that reviewed the massage parlours available in Thailand, Indonesia and Vietnam, you were advised to ask to see the girl's identification papers if age worried you. I was fairly certain that Joy wasn't younger than she said, but for all I knew she could have been fifteen or sixteen. I suppose such a thing wasn't an impossibility.

I lit a cigarette and took three tablets, washing them down with a can of Coke from the mini-bar. Joy was sitting at the mirror putting on her makeup.

'Raymond, you already have a cigarette in the ashtray,' Joy said.

I looked down at the table.

'It's on the bedside cabinet. And you need to eat something. You haven't finished your breakfast.'

I put out one of the cigarettes and glanced across at the cup of coffee and the croissant Joy had brought up for me. I felt a little nauseous and my vision was starting to blur. I went out on to the balcony to get some fresh air. The leaves of the palm trees swayed in the breeze against the blue sky, the bright chatter of an exotic bird dampened by the sound of their rustling fronds. I'd probably taken too many sleeping tablets. The feeling of nausea usually passed after a few minutes.

~

The temple garden was beautiful, bright flowering trees and shrubs hidden from the noise of the traffic. We stood holding hands by a Buddhist statue while a local government official read something from a piece of paper. We promised to love one another, to live in harmony until death, caring for one another in times of sickness. After the vows, the official congratulated us and said that I could kiss the bride.

The man from the marriage agency had come to take some photographs of the ceremony. He told us to stand in front of a tree that had pink flowers dangling from its branches. Joy wrapped her hands around my arm, hugging me to her body. When the man from the agency had finished taking photographs, we left the temple garden and shook hands with him. The government official had already left.

'What now?' I asked.

Joy laughed at me. 'I don't know. Should we go for a walk along the beach?'

'Why not.'

We crossed the beach road and walked across the sand to the edge of the sea.

'Maybe I should come and live here,' I said. 'In Thailand.'

Joy smiled. 'But what about your friends and family?'

'I don't really have any friends or family. I sometimes meet up with a colleague after work, but I don't really know much about him. I've never met his wife or been to his house.'

We made our way over to one of the beach bars and ordered two bottles of Beer Thai. I felt as though I should celebrate my second marriage. Maybe I could buy myself one of the white coral necklaces I'd seen for sale on the tourist stalls.

'Should we go for a swim in the sea?' I asked.

'I don't want to get my hair wet. But you can if you want to. I'll stay here and watch.'

'I suppose I don't feel like it either.'

I smoked a cigarette in silence. I wanted to lie on my sofa in front of the television and catch up on the programmes I'd missed. I was looking forward to going to my favourite take-away for a pizza and fries with mayonnaise and chilli sauce. In fact, it was going to be a little strange without Vincent, at least until Joy moved in. I was used to having him around, even if I didn't like taking him for walks.

'What are you thinking about?' Joy asked.

'Nothing.'

'I thought that you might be thinking about your father . . .'

'No. I was just thinking that it'll be a little strange without Vincent.'

Joy looked down at the table top, running her finger over a crack in the plastic. 'Poor Vincent. It makes me sad. You should go and ask for him back. I've told you that I'll take him for walks if you don't want to.'

'It's impossible to ask for him back. I'm not allowed to have pets in my apartment.'

I smiled and shrugged my shoulders. Hopefully I would be able to find something to watch on the television in my hotel room. I finished my bottle of Beer Thai and looked across the beach. The temperature had lowered and a wind had started to rattle the metal roofs of the beach bars, whipping at the leaves of the palm trees.

The darkening sky had turned the sea a dull grey and the beach had started to empty as the first flash of lightning forked across the sky, illuminating the coast and followed almost im-mediately by a crack of thunder that rumbled through the streets. Somewhere nearby, a car alarm started to blare, the noise muffled by the heavy rain clattering against the corrugated tin roof above our heads.

'Maybe we should go back to the hotel,' Joy said.

I edged sideways in my plastic chair away from the drops of rain that had started to leak through the tin roof. This time the lightning was closer, somewhere out of sight, a bright blue light flickering across the beach like a broken neon bulb. Someone was laughing and screaming. I looked at the sea and waited for the thunder.

15

My FATHER'S BODY had been found in an isolated villa on the coast. A long brown stain was visible on the living room floor. I found myself standing in it as I flicked through the channels on his old television, the soles of my shoes sticking to where my father's head had lain for months, presuming that he'd fallen towards the telephone.

No one had bothered to contact a specialist cleaning company. There wasn't much to clear from the villa. He'd lived there for less than a year and he clearly hadn't been planning on proving his oncologist's prognosis wrong. His possessions lay unpacked in boxes in one of the bedrooms upstairs. In the living room there was only a single chair – a green, rather ugly and badly worn leather armchair – and the old television on a stand in the corner. All the rest of the rooms were as sparsely furnished as the living room. A bare single mattress half covered with dirty blankets lay on the floor in the bedroom where he slept. In another bedroom, a wicker chair sat facing a window that overlooked the beach and the sea, the only piece of furniture in the room.

The last bottle of milk that my father had bought was still in the door of the refrigerator, the liquid separated into layers like sedimentary rock. Every time I looked at it, I pictured his body after three months of putrefaction. When I'd returned from Thailand, I'd been called to identify the body. I'd always presumed that he'd had another family. He'd been living with a woman for years, but things had clearly ended between them. The body would be lying on a steel tray in the morgue, covered by a sheet. It reminded me of a detective series on television. In a way I knew what to expect, even if the camera would usually cut away at the point where the sheet was pulled back to reveal the murder victim's face. The staff would have tried their best to clean him up a little. I couldn't help but wonder whether they'd had to pick the maggots from his corpse. But in the end I'd only been asked to identify him by the few possessions found with his body. His features had decomposed beyond recognition. In some cases a DNA test would have been required, but the detective seemed happy with things.

My father's move to the villa in the dunes seemed like a macabre joke that he'd decided to play on himself. A geological survey commissioned by the relevant authorities had concluded that the building's structure would begin to be exposed to the tides within one to two years. I'd found the report in a pile of unopened letters and electricity bills on the floor in the empty dining room. The words 'one to two years' had been underlined in an otherwise obscure paragraph.

Further along the coast, whole properties were being washed into the sea, their foundations slowly undermined by the waves. After every storm another house would be closer to collapsing on to the beach below as the loamy cliffs melted into the water. The villa's owner must have been delighted to find a buyer. The perimeter wall had been almost completely submerged by a dune. Alone in the moving domes of sand, the villa was at risk of being buried long before the sea came to lap at the door. But I supposed that it made no difference. A year was as distant as a century to a man with less than six months to live.

I stood with a cup of coffee at the sliding doors in the living room as the cleaning fluid I'd bought dissolved the stain that had leaked through the carpet to the wooden floorboards. What must once have been the garden was now an inclined expanse of sand enclosed by three white walls. Marram grass blew on the tops of the dunes beyond. The sea wasn't far away. I could hear it through the open doors.

It was a pity that Joy couldn't come to the funeral. Although my mother hadn't attended, I would have liked to have introduced her to my relatives. I hadn't seen any of them since I was a child. My aunts and uncles were getting old. Even my cousins were getting old. I couldn't help but stare at the wrinkles that had appeared around their eyes and mouths. A few of them had clearly had cosmetic surgery of one kind or another. After the burial, we went for a drink and I sat and listened to them reminisce about their childhoods with my father. Their stories didn't take long to peter out. Everyone was keen to get going. It had been a long drive and we wanted to miss the traffic on the way home.

I didn't bother to tell anyone about Joy. Some of the mourners knew that I'd been on holiday in Thailand at the time of my father's death. They asked me what it had been like and whether I'd enjoyed myself. Beyond that there wasn't much to say. No one knew why my father had decided to move into the villa. No one had ever visited him there.

16

I WAS LOOKING forward to renovating the villa by myself.
Of course, I would have to read a few books on the subject,
make a list of the tools I would need to buy. Above all, Joy
said that she wanted each of the rooms to look modern, like
the hotel we'd stayed in – especially the seating area opposite
the reception desk.

The local supermarket had a section of monthly magazines
dedicated to the subject of home improvement. In one of the
magazines, I found an article featuring a couple in their forties
who'd decided to buy an old dilapidated farmhouse in northern France. Marc, the husband, intended to dig out a small
lake in one of the fields so that he could set up a trout fishing
holiday business aimed at the Japanese market. His wife,
Gillian, would be responsible for managing the bed and breakfast side of the business.

Over the course of three months the magazine would report
on Marc and Gillian's progression as they renovated their
farmhouse and attempted to make friends in the local community. A photograph showed them chipping the old plaster from
the walls. The entire farmhouse would have to be re-wired to
modern standards if they intended to use the property as a
hotel. Already Marc and Gillian had been invited to a small
gathering by the local builder they had contracted to help with
the wiring and plumbing. A second photograph taken at night

showed a group of smiling locals sitting around a large table outside a restaurant in the village square. The Belgian couple raised their glasses with their new friends, their faces glowing softly from the light cast by a dozen candles scattered across the rustic wooden table.

I was particularly looking forward to reading about the fishing lake. Marc was having difficulty in finding a breeder with suitable trout experience, not to mention the plants he would have to buy to keep the water oxygenated to a sufficient level. Gillian's preparations for the traditional French menu would probably be a little less difficult; everything she needed would be provided by various catering suppliers, unless she intended to use a more sustainable approach and to source each product locally. But I was still interested to see which dishes she would include on her menu. Perhaps there would be a recipe I could learn. On the whole I liked Gillian a lot.

17

JOY HAD MADE two porn films within a week of her first audition in Belgium. Both had been low budget productions with neither a script or any kind of plot. In the first, she was simply filmed being fucked on a bed by the guy that had hired her – and for some of the time by the assistant cameraman. In the second film, she was joined by another woman who was told to pull Joy around by the hair and to spit on her tits.

The fact that she was from Thailand was her unique selling point. But the most obvious thing seemed to be to appear as though you loved nothing more than to fuck like a demented animal. Joy said that some of the girls were simply incapable of hiding the fact that they hated to suck a cock immediately after it had been pulled out of another girl's anus.

In less than a month we drove to Poland together for her first feature film. The script was virtually impossible to understand and seemed to have been written by a pretentious amnesiac. Perhaps it was meant to be a crime thriller: as far as I could tell there seemed to be some kind of female mafia boss who spoke with a Russian accent.

But at least I was allowed to sit and watch from a corner of the studio during the filming. I'd certainly never seen anyone fucked so hard in any of the clubs I'd been to. I couldn't resist going to the toilet to masturbate. The professionals were expected to be able to maintain an erection for hours on end while cameras and lighting rigs were being dismantled and moved around the set; and finally to ejaculate within seconds of being given the instruction by the director. In short, it was a job like any other, with certain professional considerations.

On the way back to Belgium we stayed for a night at the Paradise resort on the outskirts of Düsseldorf. A barbecue had been organised in one of the fields where customers were allowed to pitch tents. I found myself talking to an African called Charles queuing at the burger stand, a geography teacher who had left Liberia at the age of twelve after his mother had been killed in the civil war. He introduced me to his Estonian wife Lydia, and we went back to their chalet and Charles and I both penetrated her vagina at the same time while Joy took photos on her mobile phone.

18

It would have been possible to live for an entire year at the villa without ever hearing a single human voice. Only the sounds of the sea and the wind and the calls of the birds disturbed the silence.

I didn't have the energy to continue with the renovations. During the day, I watched television and wandered from room to room in my pyjama trousers. Sometimes I sat at the bedroom window upstairs and looked at the sea and the empty beach and the marram grass blowing across the dunes.

Joy must have been a little worried about me. I hadn't replied to her text messages and I'd crashed my car on the way back from Leuven. My face was cut and bruised and my chest hurt, but other than that I'd escaped relatively unharmed. No one had been seriously injured. Perhaps I'd been taking too many tablets.

I was sitting watching television when she knocked on the door. I didn't know what to do. I muted the volume and listened. After a few minutes she knocked again, a little louder. Eventually, she called my name and asked if I was alright. I didn't want her to see me in such a state. I hadn't shaved or washed and my pyjama trousers were brown with dirt. I decided to pretend that I'd been busy in the garden.

When I opened the door she looked annoyed, perhaps even a little disgusted with me.

'What have you been doing?' Joy asked.

'I didn't hear you. I've been in the garden.'

'What's happened to your face?' Joy leaned forward to look at the cuts on my forehead.

'I crashed my car. It's nothing.'

'Why didn't you call me? I've been worried about you.'

'I'm sorry. I just wanted to be alone.'

'Why? Have I done something wrong?'

'Of course not.' I tried to smile. 'I've been to the doctors . . . I'll come and see you next weekend. We can do something together.'

'I came to spend the night with you, Raymond. I've missed you.' I thought about saying sorry again, but instead I just waited for her to leave. When she'd reached the gate I closed the door and went upstairs to watch from one of the bedroom windows. A taxi was waiting for her on the road by the edge of the trees. Joy struggled through the sand in her heels, glancing up in the car's direction, her arms arching stiffly to catch her balance as she made her way across the drift of a dune. The driver clearly hadn't been willing to take the risk of driving down to the villa.

Joy reached the waiting car and emptied the sand from her shoes before climbing into the rear passenger seat. After a brief pause the car pulled away and disappeared through the trees. The indentations left in the sand by her high heels were already beginning to disappear, their outlines smoothed by the wind. Tomorrow, nothing would be visible of the route she'd taken to the villa.

A bomb had exploded on a busy street in the middle of the afternoon. The news channels were showing the same loops of recorded footage: twisted metal and smouldering black lumps of clothing and unidentifiable body parts; crying men and women; children being rushed into hospital on ambulance stretchers.

I flicked between the news channels and the music channels. A blonde police officer was bending over and rotating her buttocks, exposing the red lace of her panties. A street protest had escalated into a violent riot. A woman was pouring water over her breasts whilst playing a trumpet. I stared absently at the screen, my eyes barely focused on an advertisement for a new pet-friendly vacuum cleaner.

It was three o'clock in the morning. Joy was probably in bed. I went into the kitchen and put a meal-for-one into the microwave, one from the Italian range, tagliatelle with wild boar sausage and parmesan. The kitchen looked disgusting. The sink was piled with plates and dishes and the bin was overflowing with half-eaten microwave meals. The remnants of a chicken curry were rotting on the floor. A few nights earlier, I'd seen a rat disappear behind the fridge as I turned on the light. There was probably a nest of them. I would have to buy some poison from the supermarket. Perhaps I could call a pest control officer. He would bring specialist equipment, a machine to fumigate the nest with chemicals.

I turned the volume up on the television and flicked through the adult channels. Twenty had been provided as part of the television package that my father had subscribed to. I presumed that the money was still going out of his account. A woman in a rubber nurse's uniform was being penetrated by two men. The camera focused on her face as the men inserted their fingers into her mouth, stretching her lips and smearing her lipstick across her cheeks. I finished my meal for one and thought about masturbating, but the sky was beginning to lighten and I'd already taken too many sleeping tablets. It was almost impossible to get to sleep when the birds were singing.

19

'IT'S A LOVELY day.'
I didn't say anything.

The woman smiled and looked out across the beach to the sea, adjusting her hair in the breeze and shielding her eyes from the sun as she turned back to watch me.

'I'd give you a hand, but I probably wouldn't be much use.'

'I can manage.'

I pushed the spade into the mound of sand by the edge of the wall and shovelled it over my shoulder.

'When did you move in?'

'A few months ago.'

'I noticed it was empty. I sometimes used to see the old man that lived here.'

I looked up at the woman. She was talking about my father. The woman raised her head and waited for me to say something, but I couldn't think of anything to say.

'He hadn't been here long himself,' the woman said.

'No.'

'Did you know him then?'

'He was my father, but . . . I didn't know him very well.'

The woman lowered her hand from her eyes and looked at the sand around her feet. 'I wouldn't have guessed that you were related. You don't look anything like him.'

'I don't really know what he looked like,' I said.

'I mean . . . well, perhaps around the eyes you do.'

I lay the spade in the sand and straightened my back. The pain was incredible and the palms of my hands had already started to blister. I'd never found it necessary to learn how to use a spade. I was probably doing something wrong. There would be a certain technique to acquire.

'I'm sorry if I've offended you.'

I lit a cigarette.

'You haven't.'

I didn't know who the woman was and I wanted her to go away. She noticed me hesitate and for a second I thought that she was going to say something, but instead she did a strange thing with her mouth, exposing her teeth and frowning a little. Perhaps she had some kind of medical condition – her eyes seemed to move about a lot, as though she wasn't able to look at one thing for very long.

'Did he die, then?' the woman asked. 'Your father, I mean?'

'Yes. He had cancer.'

'I saw the ambulance. It got stuck in the sand. They didn't seem in much of a rush to dig it out.'

I stared out at the sea and smoked my cigarette. The woman watched the movement of my arm and stared at my hand and at the cigarette between my fingers. She seemed preoccupied with something. I picked up the spade and looked at my hands. My palms were red and sweating and one of the blisters had burst. I would have to buy a tube of antiseptic cream at the supermarket pharmacy. It would mean calling for a taxi. The last taxi driver they'd sent had talked for nearly the entire journey.

'Have you hurt your hand?' the woman asked.

'It's a blister.'

She nodded her head and frowned a little. 'They keep saying they're going to find a cure for it.'

'For what?'

'Cancer.'

I turned my back to the woman and continued to shovel the sand away from the wall. I'd had the chance to go back into the villa when I'd seen her walking along the beach, even as she'd turned from the sea and started to make her way towards me. I threw a spade of wet sand over my shoulder and the woman wandered over to a small patch of marram grass, her fingers pinching the hem of her cotton dress as it rippled against her breasts and hips in the breeze.

'So what are you planning to do? Are you going to sell it?'

'No. Nothing.'

'It was up for sale for a few years before your father bought it. I think the owners had given up. They don't even bother trying to sell their houses further up the coast where the worst of it is.'

'No.'

'I wonder what made him waste his money? The insurance companies are refusing to pay out.'

'I don't know. Maybe he liked the view.'

'I suppose he knew . . . that he was . . .' The woman shook her head and looked at me, smiling warmly to show that she understood my father's dying wishes.

'He came to an action group meeting once. We all felt a bit sorry for him, but he made an excuse and left after twenty minutes. There were only two or three of us there, so I don't think we made much of an impression. You would think there would be more of a community spirit. I mean, there are things the council could be doing, but they're just blaming everything on the government. If you want to, you can come to a meeting. . . ?'

I shrugged my shoulders. I didn't know what to say.

'But you're going to lose everything. There are things we could be doing.'

The woman hesitated, her tongue angrily wetting her bottom lip. 'I'm sorry. I'll leave you alone. I just wanted to say hello.'

I nodded and continued shovelling the sand away from the perimeter wall as the woman made her way through the dunes towards the sea. It had taken me all afternoon to move less than half of the mound. In parts it was over ten feet deep. A little further away where the marram grass had taken root, trees had been planted in an attempt to bind the sand into soil – rows of now long-dead saplings surrounded by a rusty wire fence, their dry branches rasping in the wind.

I looked across at the flat expanse of the beach as a dozen gulls fought in the air above a stretch of water left by the tide. The woman had disappeared beyond the dunes and the light was beginning to soften and fade. It was almost dark by the time I'd finished moving the mound of sand away from the perimeter wall. The pain in my hands was unbearable and it was impossible for me to straighten my fingers without opening up the loose skin from the large blisters that had formed across my palms.

After locking the gate, I washed my hands at the kitchen sink and looked in the cupboard underneath for a tube of antiseptic cream. Scattered mounds of rat faeces had started to accumulate amongst the various bottles and spray cans of cleaning fluid and insect killer. The nest was probably in the wall or under the floor. I'd made an effort to remove the bags of rubbish from the kitchen, but the worktops were still covered with dirty plates and half-eaten microwave meals. The large black pellets retained a sheen of moisture for days. After a week they started to lose their colour and to fade to a greying powder. I tried my best to ignore them, but I found it hard not to look for fresh droppings while I waited for the microwave to heat a meal-for-one. I'd considered pouring a kettle of

boiling water into the hole behind the refrigerator. I wanted to
hear the little fuckers scream as they died in agony.

20

J OY HAD BOUGHT her first car – a relatively old yellow
Citroën that she loved. I hadn't known that she could drive.
Perhaps she'd been taking driving lessons in Leuven.

I waved and smiled, out of breath from the walk across the
sand to the road, glancing through the passenger window as I
opened the door at the turquoise leopard-print mini-skirt she
was wearing.

'You look amazing,' I said, leaning across to kiss her as I
fastened my seatbelt.

'Thank you.' She offered me her cheek and kissed the air to
the side of my face as I pressed my lips to the hollow beneath
her cheekbone.

'How are things? You look as though you've lost weight?'

'Yeah, a little. I've been really busy with work.'

'How's it going then?'

'Good. Really good. I'm really enjoying it.'

'I'd forgotten that we'd arranged to go out until you sent a
text message to me this morning.' I lit a cigarette and looked
through the window at the sea as we followed the coast road
through the pine trees.

'Hold it out of the window. I don't want my clothes to
smell.'

'We should go to a seafood restaurant.'

'We've already made arrangements.'

'Where for?'

'An Italian. Blow your smoke out of the window. Wind it down all the way.'

We turned from the coast road and followed the signs for the motorway. Within an hour we were on the outskirts of Brussels.

'So what are their names?'

'Diana and Jan. I've told you their names.'

'I know you have. I'd forgotten them.'

I looked at the apartment blocks and brightly lit car show-rooms in the evening light. On the phone Joy had told me that her new friends were a relatively well-known couple in the Netherlands and that they'd managed to move from starring in and directing porn films to appearing on late-night television. I'd made sure to sound enthusiastic. But I didn't know how I was going to cope with the general flow of the conversation. Perhaps I would have been able to cancel if I'd said that the pest control officer had insisted on coming at eight p.m. on Saturday, or that it was going to take all weekend for him to deal with the rat infestation.

Before I hung up, Joy had reminded me to make sure that I shaved my scrotum in case we were invited back to the cou-ple's apartment. The last time we'd gone to a club I hadn't made much of an effort and a woman lying on a raised plat-form in the centre of a gangbang had pushed me away as I'd knelt over her face. Joy had been lying next to the woman, her splayed legs pointing in the opposite direction. The woman was well-known in the club – a lawyer who held parties on a river boat and regularly lashed out at the club's male clientele if they edged the tips of their cocks towards her face without first seeking the glance of her approval. Since she'd had one hand on Joy's pussy, I'd mistakenly thought that it would be acceptable to offer her my cock. She knew I was with Joy, but perhaps I'd invaded her personal space a little too aggressively. Some women preferred you to stand a few metres away, quietly masturbating for five or ten minutes before making a slow, incremental approach, as obsequious as a field zoologist creeping to the nest of a mountain gorilla. But Joy thought the lawyer had pushed me away because I hadn't shaved my pubic hair.

If I were to write of the evening, perhaps for a couple review on PARTNERS.BE, I would describe Jan as a nice guy with a big cock, friendly and relaxed. With Diana it would be necessary to summarise her love of sucking cock; but more than anything, two cocks in her pussy and a dildo up her arse were the most preferable of situations.

After a glass of wine I started to find it a little easier to join in the conversation at the table. I was regretting not making more of an effort with my appearance. I hadn't shaved for days and my shirt wasn't ironed very well. I felt that I needed to reassure Diana that I'd shaved my scrotum before leaving the house. It was obvious that their own personal hygiene would be of the highest standards. I tried to think of a way to introduce the subject of personal grooming, but Jan wanted to talk about home improvements.

'Joy said you've bought a villa, Raymond?' Jan glanced down at his plate of salad leaves, his fork circling limply from the tips of his fingers.

'It was my father's. I'm just doing the renovation. I thought it would be good if we could spend the weekends there.'

'Yeah. By the sea. We bought an old farmhouse a few years ago. We had to pretty much gut the place. But it was worth the trouble. I mean, it looks amazing now. We had a glass wall installed overlooking a beautiful wood – you know with the brushed aluminium frame? And we love the peace and quiet.

I've even bought two cows. I'm going to learn how to make cheese.'

I nodded and smiled politely as I slid a piece of chicken across my plate. Joy was by far the more attractive of the two women. Diana looked like a typical porn star: hair bleached almost white, enormous silicone breast implants, swollen Botox-injected lips and the kind of hideous retroussé nose worn by Michael Jackson, a mini rhino horn of reconstructed cartilage. She looked like a total fucking idiot slut and I wanted desperately to stick my cock in her. Perhaps that was the idea. As the waiter came to clear away our plates, I realised that I was going to have to sit through the rest of the meal with an erection.

After dinner we went back to Jan and Diana's apartment in the city. It was an enjoyable evening: Jan was a nice guy, friendly and relaxed; and Diana obviously loved sucking cock. I sat on the couch next to Jan while Diana knelt between my legs and sucked my cock and Joy knelt between Jan's legs and sucked his cock. After that we swapped positions and Diana and Joy spread their legs while Jan and I knelt on the floor and licked their vaginas.

Diana said that she really loved having two cocks fucking her pussy at the same time, so Jan lay on top of the glass coffee table and Diana straddled him and lay forwards to allow me to push my cock into her vagina above her husband's cock. I had visions of the coffee table shattering and a shard of glass slicing through somebody's neck, but Jan said not to worry, that you could hit the glass with a hammer and it still wouldn't break.

Joy seemed happy just to watch, spreading her legs on the armchair and wetting her fingers with saliva as she parted her labia and rubbed her clitoris. After I'd come I put on my jeans and went out on to the balcony for a cigarette while Jan fucked

Joy and Diana went to the bathroom. I'd noticed a small smear of blood on my condom and Diana was worried that she'd torn her vaginal wall again.

A soft rain was falling and a milky dome of light arched in the sky above the city. I took a long drag and exhaled a cloud of smoke at the grey buildings as I leant against the aluminium rail. I couldn't help but picture myself falling head first into the nothingness. Joy had started to moan loudly, her voice muffled by the glass and the rain and the sound of the traffic. I looked through the sliding door. Jan was still fucking her, his hands holding her ankles in the air. Diana was standing beside the armchair, her lips moving silently as her face formed into a series of exaggerated expressions. I finished my cigarette and threw the stub over the balcony railing, watching its trajectory down towards the concrete pavement below.

I slid open the balcony door and went to stand by Joy's side, caressing her left breast and watching Jan's cock sliding in and out of her pussy. She had a pretty vagina, as pretty as any I'd ever seen. Diana's had obviously needed a little work – she'd clearly had her inner labia trimmed and the opening to her vagina tightened.

'How are you?' I asked Diana, noticing that she'd put on a pair of grey jogging pants and a T-shirt.

'I'm fine. It's nothing.' She shrugged her shoulders, perhaps a little annoyed with the failure of her body. 'That's what happens when you have children.'

I nodded and leant forwards to rub Joy's clitoris, the tips of my fingers glancing against Jan's penis as I lowered my mouth to Joy's breasts. Diana knelt on the other side of the armchair, reaching around to play with her husband's testicles. When Joy had come Jan climbed up on to the arms of the chair, squatting over her face and ejaculating violently into her mouth as his wife caressed his pulsing anus.

I sat on the sofa and watched a news channel on television while Joy went to the bathroom to wipe her face. A man wearing a green shirt was talking to a reporter outside an office block. On the screen it said that four hundred people had been killed in an earthquake. Jan was sitting out of breath in the armchair, his forehead dripping with sweat. On the wall behind him there was a large black and white photograph of their son, taken two or three weeks after his birth. Dramatically lit, with areas of deep shadow, the naked baby was held in Jan's muscular arms in an imitation of the horrible poster young women used to hang on their bedroom walls. The framing and lighting used in the photograph suggested a comparison with the infant Christ – a modern retelling of the immaculate conception in which the virgin Mary is employed in the adult film industry.

21

MY FATHER HAD taken to cultivating a bonsai tree during his last years. It was a hobby that required little physical effort and therefore suitable for a sick man lacking in energy. The miniature tree sat in an ornamental porcelain dish on the windowsill in the smallest bedroom in the villa, faced by a wicker armchair whose sides were fraying and punctured with holes, the only furniture in the room. I hadn't paid much attention to the room. It was as bare and as dusty as the rest, and I'd mistaken the bonsai tree for a shrivelled, dying plant that had found itself deposited and ignored in a spare bedroom.

On the floor beneath the window, a black wooden box contained the specialist tools my father had used to prune and cultivate the tree. Each tool was small and precise, with delicately carved wooden handles and polished steel blades fashioned into incomprehensible shapes. I'd considered taking up the hobby myself, but the box of obscure tools suggested a certain amount of intricacy. Occasionally, I would sit in the wicker chair and look at the tree, trimming a leaf or snipping the tip of a branch with the secateurs, feeding the soil a drop of water from the long spout of an elaborate brass watering can. It was remarkable to look at, a miniature imitation of a wizened cherry blossom tree whose trunk and branches had been weathered by a century of mountain winds. I half-expected a finger-sized samurai to step out from behind the tree, furiously hacking at the air with his matchstick sword, angered by my impertinence to sit and stare.

I had no idea what kind of person would be attracted to a hobby requiring decades of dedication to a single plant whose changes were almost imperceptible. Even the youngest leaves hadn't grown in a month. But I liked to sit and look at the bonsai tree, at the dunes and the sea, perhaps like my father; the small, empty room had its own quiet atmosphere. The villa was in the same state of disrepair and neglect that it had been in when I'd first looked around. Perhaps things were getting even worse. A leaking tap in the bathroom had seized; I'd broken the fridge pouring boiling water on to a rat as it tried to escape into the wall; the living room door had jammed shut and I'd had to kick it open.

Once or twice I'd leafed through an old copy of the Yellow Pages with the idea of finding a builder to do all the necessary work, but the edition I'd found was over ten years old. The companies listed would have changed their telephone numbers or closed down entirely. Google offered millions of local building company results. I looked at the first page and gave up. Most people asked their friends and family to recommend a good local builder, or even their work colleagues. Perhaps I could ask Joy to ask Jan and Diana.

The kitchen was beginning to disgust me. I had to leave the TV turned on so that I didn't have to listen to the rats. I'd carried the microwave into the living room so I could heat a meal for one without having to go into the kitchen. I was thinking about setting fire to the cupboards and the broken refrigerator and leaving the room to burn down to its concrete shell. But there was a risk that someone would see the smoke and call the fire brigade. There would be an investigation and the case would be considered for prosecution on the grounds that I'd wasted the time of the emergency services. I would have to make sure the fire looked like an accident. It would be a good idea to get slightly injured so that it looked like I'd made an effort to put out the flames.

Concealing the injury from Joy wouldn't be too complicated. She'd said that she was worried about me, but I hadn't spoken to her for weeks. If she rang my mobile phone I usually pretended to have missed the call. I don't know why. It just seemed easier that way. To reassure her I told her that I'd applied for a job with a Korean electronics manufacturer in Leuven and that I was waiting for them to reply to my email.

But no one had emailed me for months. I'd considered closing my email account, but I found a certain amount of pleasure in deleting the hundreds of spam messages I received every day. PARTNERS.BE had reminded me that my premium membership was about to expire. I had no intention of renewing my subscription. Joy had asked me to remove the photographs I'd uploaded of her, and so no one would bother to contact me any more. Besides, I was happy just to masturbate before I went to sleep. Sometimes I would wander through the dunes towards the nature reserve. On warm summer evenings local men would organise gangbangs for their wives in the dunes further east, but I'd only ever found used condoms. After an hour of walking aimlessly, I would sit in the sand before heading back to the villa.

PART TWO

22

THE BODY HAD been found by a man walking his dog. That's how the bodies of murdered young women are found. By men walking their dogs.

I was arrested at six o'clock in the morning by two detectives. When I didn't answer the door, a uniformed policeman broke it open. The detectives found me lying on the mattress in the bedroom. One of them shook me by the shoulder and asked me whether my name was Raymond Verleaux. When I said 'yes' the detective told me that he was arresting me for murder. I didn't know what to say. I'd taken some sleeping tablets and I felt a little confused.

One of the detectives told me to get dressed, and when I said that I was already dressed he pulled back my duvet and looked down at the dirty jeans and the stained T-shirt I was wearing. I was in the habit of going to bed in my clothes.

'Get some shoes on,' the detective said. 'Put something on your feet.'

I did as I was told and followed the detectives downstairs. One of the detectives told me to stand in a corner of the living room while they had a look around. Neither of them looked like detectives. The big one had a shaved head and was wearing an Adidas tracksuit jacket. He wouldn't have looked out of place in a crowd at a football match.

'It'll be better if you tell us the truth, Raymond,' the smallest of the detectives said. They still hadn't told me their names. 'Did you hear what I said?'

I didn't know what to say. After a few minutes I asked them if they were going to take me to the police station. The detectives smiled at one another.

'Yes, we'll be taking you to the police station,' the tall detective said.

I didn't say anything. I wanted them to think that I was a nice person, even if I'd done nothing wrong. I tried my best to look helpful while the detectives looked around the room, carefully stepping through the mud that had been left by the storm. I hadn't even asked who I was supposed to have murdered. I thought about it for a minute or two.

'What are you looking for?' I asked.

'You know what we're looking for, Raymond.'

'Why don't you tell us where it is?'

'I don't know what you're looking for,' I said.

'What happened to the floor?' the small detective asked.

'There was a storm. The villa flooded.'

'We're looking for the knife you used to kill your wife.'

The detectives turned to look at me. They wanted to see how I was going to react to the news. The whole thing was confusing, but I knew that it was probably important to look shocked. It was a strange situation. I couldn't believe what was happening, and at the same time I could believe what was happening. After a few minutes, the second detective gave me a dirty look and led me by the arm to the door. I was trying to look shocked, and even though I was shocked I didn't know how to look shocked. We stopped outside the villa and the detective holding my arm said something. For some reason I thought about smiling. I hadn't heard what he'd said. But instead I just looked at the dunes in front of the villa and the police car waiting for me in the distance.

I was questioned until the early hours of the following morning. Occasionally the lawyer I'd been given would interrupt the detectives, but by the end he was too tired to say anything. When I asked for a cigarette one of the detectives told me that I wasn't allowed to smoke in the building, but that if I was suffering from nicotine withdrawal a doctor would be requested so that I could be prescribed with nicotine patches.

The only question I could remember had been about Joy's red handbag. Both of the detectives had asked me the same question, but I'd never seen Joy with a red handbag. The detectives had taken it in turns to return to the same questions over and over again. When I was getting tired they would take me back to my cell and my lawyer would bring me a cup of coffee and tell me that I was doing fine.

The cell was small and suffocating and it had a metal toilet in the corner without a sink or toilet paper. I sat on the concrete bench and stared at the walls. The halogen light in the centre of the ceiling buzzed constantly. None of the films or television programmes I'd seen had prepared me for what a police cell was really like, but I knew that it was strange to be able to take a look 'behind the scenes' like that. Most people would never get the chance to sit in a police cell and to be interviewed by two detectives. Perhaps if my arrest hadn't been so serious I would have been able to appreciate things a little more. It was strange to suddenly find yourself in such a situation.

The next day the tall detective drove me back to the villa. Five or six vans as big as motor homes with enormous satellite dishes on their roofs were parked by the side of the road. A news reporter holding a microphone turned to look at the detective's car as we pulled over and stopped. For a few seconds I wondered whether something terrible had happened, whether someone had drowned in the sea or a child's body had been found in the dunes.

The detective pulled the handbrake on and stared out through the windscreen. After a few seconds he turned to look at me. He seemed to be in a terrible mood. He hadn't spoken a word since we left the police station. I'd probably complicated things for him by refusing to admit my guilt, but I still wanted him to like me. I wanted him to know that I hadn't done anything.

'Looks like you're going to be famous, Mr Verleaux,' the detective said. Three news reporters were walking quickly towards the car. I wasn't sure whether I was allowed to get out of the car or not. I wanted to ask about Joy, but I knew that my questions would only make the detective angry again. I knew that it would be better if I said nothing.

The news reporters surrounded me as I left the detective's car, elbowing their way between six or seven cameramen. I noticed that one of the microphones pushed in front of me had the letters RTBF written on it. I looked at the woman's hand that was holding the microphone. Her fingernails had been filed and painted very neatly. Her hand looked pretty, her fingers thin and pale and a little tanned. I looked at her wrist and arm and tried to see her face, but I couldn't see anything because of the camera lights shining in my eyes.

'Did you kill your wife, Mr Verleaux?'

I shook my head and looked at the ground because of the bright camera lights. 'No. I didn't.'

'Where were you on the night of her murder?'

'I've been through all of this with the police.'

'Have you been charged yet?'

I stopped and lit a cigarette. They were taking it in turns to ask questions and it was impossible to concentrate with the lights shining in my face. The cameras made it difficult to think. I could feel them pointing at me. I put my cigarettes back in my pocket and took a long drag. My hands were shaking.

One of the reporters fell over in the sand, tripping up one of the cameramen. Everybody in front of me was trying to walk backwards. I'd seen similar things on television when something had happened to someone and it was a big news story. We stopped to let the journalist and the cameraman get back to their feet. They brushed their clothes and then got back into their positions as though they were re-taking their places after a false start in a race.

The fact that I'd lit a cigarette seemed to make the reporters angry. Someone asked if I didn't care about Joy's murder. I didn't fully hear what the question was because it had been interrupted by a question from someone else. Asking questions and walking backwards through the sand was beginning to tire the reporters. A woman from a radio station fell and lost her shoe. This time everyone managed to avoid her and we left her sitting in the sand to catch her breath. Most of the people left in front of me had decided to walk sideways or to walk looking over their shoulders. The cameramen were taking it in turns to run ahead and stand their ground as I approached, resuming their former position once I'd overtaken them.

The sand was quite deep and we were making slow progress. The road to the villa had completely disappeared. A mound of sand six feet deep and as wide as a house had blown across where I'd been able to see a piece of the road a few weeks earlier. For almost a minute no one bothered to ask any questions, but as we neared the villa the news reporters started to jostle with one another again. I made for a gap between two cameramen, taking a sudden diversion in the hope of catching them by surprise.

'Did you kill your wife, Mr Verleaux?'

'No. I didn't. I had nothing to do with it.'

'Where were you on the night of the murder, Mr Verleaux?'

'I was at home.'

'Why were you arrested?'

'I don't know.'

One of the cameramen tried to stop me from getting to the gate by standing in my way and refusing to move. I had to walk around him and push against him with my shoulder, holding out my arm to prevent him from getting in my way again. Eventually I found myself standing at the gate with the reporters and cameramen standing behind me. I took out my keys and looked at them. I couldn't figure out which was the right key. My hands were still shaking and the reporters were still asking the same questions.

As I closed the gate behind me, one of the reporters lunged forwards and asked me again if I'd killed Joy. He looked angry, like the detective had been, but perhaps his expression was only for the people watching television.

23

I T WAS STRANGE to see myself on television. I looked different to what I looked like in the mirror and in photographs.
The television cameras seemed to distort my face, to change
the shape of my skull, twisting the muscles around my mouth
and jaw. I felt as though I was watching someone else, a bad
actor pretending to be accused of murder.

The news channels had managed to get a photograph of me
from somewhere. It was usually shown at the beginning of a
report, followed by a clip of me refusing to answer questions
as I reached the villa's gate. Then the presenter would discuss
'the latest developments' with a reporter waiting 'live at the
scene'. Sometimes an expert in psychology or criminal investi-
gations would be interviewed in the studio, and the presenter
would ask them questions about my personal life. Usually
they discussed the fact that I'd been dismissed from my job
on mental health grounds and that my former colleagues had
described me as slightly strange.

I didn't turn the television off for days. The boiler had
broken and so I was able to use the television as a sort of
radiator to heat the room during the evenings. Besides, it had
started to emit a strangely pleasant melting plastic smell that
I liked. I'd moved both the television and the microwave upstairs, away from the rats and the water. I could heat a microwave meal-for-one without getting out of bed. I rarely both-

ered to get out of bed. As soon as I woke up I would turn my head towards the screen. Sometimes the first thing I saw was my own face, or rather the twisted face of the bad actor. For a few seconds I would wonder whether it had all been a dream. The same thing happened every time I woke up. Usually you would expect to sigh with relief before closing your eyes to yawn and stretch. But each time I would have to realise that it wasn't all a dream. I suppose I was starting to get used to the idea that Joy had been murdered and that I was never going to see her again.

The news channels didn't have much to report as far as the crime was concerned. They only knew that Joy's body had been found on wasteland not far from the motorway in Leuven and that she had been stabbed over fifty times in the breasts and vagina. Sometimes they would simply state that she had been stabbed repeatedly, but most of the time they liked to remind viewers that she had been stabbed over fifty times in the breasts and vagina. After a few days the words didn't seem to bother me as much. I thought that it might be important for them to say things like that to help with the police investigation. You had to think of ways to keep the public's attention. It was the same with an advertisement for washing detergent. Stabbed fifty times in the breasts and vagina stuck in your head like whiter than the whitest whites.

Eventually, a reporter standing outside an apartment building said that a thirty-four-year-old man had been arrested by detectives investigating the murder of porn star Joy Valentine. The suspect's name was Sebastien Bluot and he was described as a government administrator. A passport photograph was shown of the man. He had short brown hair and blue eyes and he was wearing a white shirt. But there was nothing remarkable about him. Perhaps you could say that his skin looked a little pale. It was easy to imagine him sitting behind a desk in a government office.

I lit a cigarette and reached to turn the kettle on, emptying a sachet of instant coffee into the bottom of a dirty cup as I waited for the water to boil. A box of my tablets was just out of reach on the floor. I thought about getting up and going to the bathroom. I felt as though I was going to vomit again. I could pick the tablets up on my way back to bed. I looked at the kettle, at the cable running from the kettle across the floor to where it was plugged into the wall socket. On top of the plug there was a small red sticker to say that the appliance had been tested by the quality control department of whichever factory it had been made in.

I changed channels with the remote control. There was a documentary about the demise of eel fishing in Kazakhstan. A fisherman called Yerzhan was rowing across a river in the dark. Each day he would check his eel nets at four in the morning. Sometimes he would catch hundreds of small elvers, the worm-like baby eels that spawn in the Sargasso Sea, and fry them alive for his breakfast. But every year things were becoming more difficult – and now it was almost impossible. The eels he'd fished with his father and grandfather were disappearing and the species had been listed as critically endangered.

I finished my cigarette and filled my cup with hot water. Yerzhan had managed to catch three small brown fish, but no eels. He pulled them from the net and dropped them into the bottom of the boat. His father and grandfather had earned a living smoking the eels they caught and selling them at the market, and so he felt a need to continue the tradition, but it was impossible to make any money. Besides, he was divorced and he didn't need much money. During the day he worked at a supermarket. Things had changed and he was happy that his daughter was in the third year of a Communication Studies degree at university.

The fisherman threw his net back into the water and rowed back to the shore. Back in his small apartment, he poured himself a glass of vodka and sat at a kitchen table covered with a square of flowered linoleum, before putting on his blue and yellow supermarket uniform and setting off to work.

I got up and went to the bathroom to vomit. On my way back to bed I picked up the box of tablets from the floor and looked out of the window. The remaining television crews and photographers had left. I lay back down on the mattress and changed channels with the remote control. The same reporter as before was standing outside the apartment building where the man accused of Joy's murder had been arrested. I looked at his photograph again, at his short brown hair and blue eyes, at the white shirt that he was wearing. After that there was a repeat of the news report investigating the government's approach to promoting healthy lifestyles.

I took four tablets. When I'd finished the half-eaten lasagne I'd left on top of a pile of TV magazines by the bed, I would allow myself to take four more tablets. It seemed a reasonable way of doing things.

24

IN THE SECOND week of April I left the villa to find a thick blanket of snow covering the garden. The snow was still falling, flakes like white moths drifting gently to the ground in the silent air.

I knew that it was snowing before I looked out of the window because it was the main news story on television. It hadn't snowed like that before, so deep, so late in April. The dunes and the beach were blanketed and the sea was a thick grey line in the whiteness. I thought that it might be nice to go for a walk, to feel the snow beneath my feet.

Someone had already been out walking their dog. Two rows of dragged footprints were heading towards the beach, followed by a more complicated pattern of dots and dashes. I stopped and looked at the footprints as they stretched out and disappeared in a long fading line. In the distance, the pine trees flickered black and grey against the white sky. It was a nice feeling to stand there in the falling snow looking at the disappearing footprints and the pine trees. I didn't move for what seemed like a long time except to raise my face a little so that I could feel the snowflakes landing on my skin.

When I got back to the villa I climbed back into bed and watched the news on television. The main report said that parts of the country were under nearly half a metre of snow and that the difficult conditions were causing traffic chaos. A police commander advised everyone to stay at home unless their journeys were absolutely necessary. I took three more tablets and waited for the weather report. Even though it was snowing, Tatiana Silva would be wearing a short skirt or a tight, sleeveless blouse.

The snow had certainly given everyone something to talk about. An administration manager in Nivelles said that he'd spoken to his neighbour for the first time in eight years because of the weather. He couldn't exactly call his neighbour a friend, they'd only spoken for perhaps two or three minutes and he'd still never been into his apartment, but it was going to be a little sad when everything returned to normal.

I used my mobile phone to take some pictures of the beach and the dunes and uploaded them on to my profile page on THAILOVELINKS.COM. I thought that Pamela might like the photos. She was a twenty-year-old student living in Bangkok and she'd accepted my friend request. It was a good idea. She replied to my message within a few hours and said that she thought the photographs were beautiful.

To continue the conversation I asked her if she'd like me to take some more photographs, perhaps of the windmill in Gistel. I don't know why I suggested the windmill in Gistel, except that I thought it would look beautiful. But this time it took Pamela more than a week to answer my second message, and by then the weather had warmed and the snow had melted to mud. Her response was a brief and indirect apology that was clearly aiming to curtail the conversation. I didn't know whether to reply or not. In the end I decided not to bother.

But I went to Gistel to see the windmill anyway. I don't know why, except that it was a warm day and I felt like doing something. It was nice to walk along the towpath by the side of the canal, slowly winding your way through the fields past farm buildings and little patches of woodland. The windmill was pretty, its bright white paint flickering in the afternoon sun behind the gentle rhythm of four trellised red sails. I took some photographs using my mobile phone and sat at a table outside an old grain house that had been converted into a little café.

It was nice just to sit and listen to the soft slow turning of the windmill's wooden gears as the sails cut through the seemingly still air. The waitress was busy with a family of cyclists at the next table. The couple's only child was clearly going to be allowed to choose something from the menu for itself, each hesitation and change of mind indulged by the happy, smiling parents.

I looked at the photographs I'd taken of the windmill on my mobile phone and pretended to check my text messages. No one had contacted me for months. Perhaps it had even been a year. I couldn't remember. Even my friend Bernard had stopped replying to my text messages. For a few months I'd been considering trying to start a conversation with one of the assistants at the supermarket pharmacy. But in the end I didn't bother. Besides, there was always the internet.

When the waitress had finished with the family of cyclists she came over to my table and took my order. She was pretty, perhaps in her early twenties, and had an eastern European accent.

'I hope you don't mind me saying, but I think I recognise you from television . . .' She bit her lip and thought for a moment. 'Were you married to the porn star that was murdered?'

I nodded my head. 'Yes.'

'My boyfriend really liked her. She was his favourite porn star. It was really sad when she was murdered.'

I nodded my head again. 'Thank you.'

When the waitress had left I found myself staring at a small sign staked into the grass by the entrance to the café, informing tourists of the Oostmolen windmill museum's opening hours and the possibility of a guided tour. The family of cyclists had fallen silent. I didn't know whether they'd heard what the waitress had said or not. I tried my best to look normal and took out my mobile phone again, checking my empty inbox for the second time. Perhaps it wouldn't be too humiliating to pretend to compose a text message to someone. I clicked the compose a text message button and stared at the empty white screen and the flashing black line waiting for me to write something. After a few seconds I clicked on the internet service provider icon, pausing before deciding to delete the spam messages from my email account. Hundreds of messages offered penis-enhancement drugs and dates with cock-loving sluts. I clicked on an email from 'Lauren in California'. There was a photograph of a naked blonde woman splaying her labia and a link to a dating website.

'Hey sexy! Wanna play with me tonight? My soaking wet pussy is waiting for your cock.'

I looked at her tanned skin and her blue eyes, her darkened nipples and labia. Someone a few tables away was talking about the story in the news about a thirteen-year-old girl being gang-raped at school by her classmates. The man's voice was coming from somewhere just behind me. Whoever he was sitting with didn't seem to be saying anything. I could only hear the same quiet and monotonous voice.

The family of cyclists were already getting up to leave by the time I'd deleted most of the spam messages from my email account. I hadn't even noticed them eating. I started to worry that I'd been talking to myself again. The waitress seemed to have been paying me a certain amount of attention. At first I'd thought it was because her boyfriend owned some of Joy's DVDs.

I smiled inanely and waited to catch the waitress's attention before I left.

'Tell your boyfriend that it would have meant a lot to Joy . . . For people to have enjoyed her DVDs.'

'Of course.' She paused and nodded before disappearing with her tray to the kitchen.

On the opposite bank in the shade of a stone bridge further along the canal, a man in his early sixties wearing a large cream-coloured fedora was sitting painting the windmill from behind a wooden easel. An elderly couple and a man with a dog had gathered on the bridge to watch the painter as he worked. They smiled enthusiastically at one another, nodding their heads in appreciation.

I stopped on my way back to the bus stop and the elderly couple moved a little to allow me to see over the painter's shoulder.

'It's beautiful, isn't it?' the elderly woman remarked, the buttery skin of her face melting in the warm glow of nostalgia cast by the canvas. For some reason the painter had decided to paint the scene as it might have appeared almost a hundred years ago. But it was hard to guess exactly which decade had been chosen. A horse-drawn barge was being pulled along the canal in the foreground, its windows glowing orange and yellow from the heat of a coal fire and its little chimney puffing with smoke in the evening air. Yet on the country road that passed over the bridge a ruby-coloured Citroën van from the early 1950s was about to disappear between blossoming hedgerows.

The man with the small fat dog edged slowly away, leaving the bridge by a path that cut through the fields while the elderly couple discussed making an offer to buy the painting. It was the type of painting whose limited edition signed prints were sold in the Galerie d'Art in the shopping mall on Rue Neuve. A world without televisions or computers; a simple life of butchers' shops and bakeries, of quiet rain-wet streets and the smell of dampened wood smoke.

25

P AMELA STILL HADN'T replied to me on THAILOVE-
LINKS.COM. I'd left her a message telling her that I'd uploaded some photographs I'd taken of the windmill in Gistel.
I thought about de-friending her again and allowed the mouse
cursor to hover over the 'Remove' button for several minutes.
Her profile photograph looked reasonably professional; shot
from a low angle to accentuate the length of her legs, she was
standing in a modern apartment wearing a very short mini-
dress and high heels.

I stared at the small image, at the light sheen of Pamela's
calf and ankle and the tight hem of her dress. An LED on my
laptop started to flash, indicating that the battery was running
low. Within a few minutes a warning message would instruct
me to connect to a power supply. The living room had flooded
during the night and the electricity supply had been cut. Sea
water turned black with dirt floated a scum of detritus halfway
up the stairs. If I wanted to leave the villa I would have to
climb from the balcony on to the terrace and then make my
way along the perimeter wall.

I didn't know what I was going to do when it started to go
dark outside. It would be impossible to watch television or to
heat a meal-for-one in the microwave. I would have to eat a
cold spaghetti in Bolognese sauce.

Marie was in the chatroom at PARTNERS.BE. I asked her

how her day had been and she said OK. We usually talked a
lot about things but she didn't seem as though she was in the
mood. Her boyfriend had been messing her about a lot re-
cently. I didn't know where Marie lived exactly but she'd told
me that her boyfriend worked in an office in Mechelen and so
I presumed that she lived in Mechelen. I understood why she
didn't want to tell me where she lived. It was better to be safe
about things like that. At first she'd been reluctant to tell me
her name. Her username on PARTNERS.BE was HornyGirl21.
I still didn't know her surname. There was probably no reason
for me to ask.

Marie had uploaded some new photographs that her boyfriend had taken at a recent gangbang. I always made the effort
to give her photographs five stars, even if they weren't particularly interesting. We were good friends and I liked talking to
her. She was funny and intelligent. Sometimes we would talk
until three or four in the morning when the chatroom had virtually emptied. Marie could hold conversations with four or
five men at the same time on a series of subjects, but after
a couple of hours most of the men would get bored and we
would be left alone together. Occasionally, Marie would masturbate for me on her webcam. She had a beautiful vagina and
she would fuck herself with the remote control for the television or one of her cans of hairspray.

At the moment she was discussing the gangbang she'd re-
cently been to with someone in the chatroom. There'd been
eight men in total, all of them black. The photographs were
more or less the usual sort of thing. The identical black ski
masks worn by each of the men had probably been provided
by Marie's boyfriend to save him the effort of blurring the
men's faces before he uploaded the photographs on to PART-
NERS.BE, even though some of the men were clearly married.
Perhaps it had been a requirement for participants to provide

their own ski masks. I supposed that it would be preferable to being asked to wear a condom. They should have considered themselves fortunate in that regard.

The thought of having a penis enlargement still occurred to me occasionally. I'd managed to gain just over half an inch in length as a teenager by adopting a kind of stretching device invented by my friend using an old rubber inner tube from a bicycle tyre. I'd never much cared about the size of my penis after marrying Anthea, but it was clearly the only way I was going to get anywhere with anyone like Marie. One of the photographs showed her being vaginally penetrated by two masked men at the same time, while another two forced their cocks into her mouth. I clicked on the next of the photographs. This time she was kneeling on the floor as three of the men ejaculated into her mouth and across her face. In another she was bent over on the bed as two of the men ejaculated across her vagina and anus, blurring her labia in a thick veil of opaque, greying semen.

Marie was still in the chatroom. I told her that I liked the photographs she'd uploaded. I knew that she hadn't immediately seen what I'd written because it took a few minutes for her to respond. Eventually, she said thank you, and that she was looking forward to her next gangbang at the weekend. I considered telling her that I'd decided to have a penis extension but she seemed to be in a conversation with a single woman called PussyLicker69.

Scrolling back through their conversation, I saw that Marie had invited PussyLicker69 to a BDSM night being held at a club called Occasions in Brussels. I clicked on to Pussy-Licker69's profile page. She described herself as a 'bisexual law student based in the beautiful and historic city of Liège'. Her breasts were small and beautiful, as soft and white as snow, her nipples the colour of bruised peaches in the dim light of a student bedroom. Somewhat unusually, considering her age, in one photograph PussyLicker69 had allowed her pubic hair to grow into a thick tangle of little black curls that thinned to flattened wisps across her inner thighs and buttocks, reaching past her anus to the tip of her coccyx. I often presumed that a hairy vagina would smell much stronger than usual. But I didn't know. I couldn't remember ever encountering a hairy vagina.

When PussyLicker69 left the chatroom I tried to think of something interesting to say to Marie. But it was impossible and within a few minutes she'd already started a conversation with somebody else. I stared at the screen, watching their words appear and disappear, barely bothering to read what they were saying. I suppose I could have tried to join in the conversation, but I didn't see the point. The battery in my computer was about to go. The warning light was beginning to fade and I was sitting waiting for my computer screen to go black.

26

I'D BECOME SOMETHING of a minor celebrity since Joy's murder, even if the waitress in Gistel had been the only person to recognise me. A publishing company had approached me with the idea of writing a book about her and I'd been invited on to a daytime chat show on television.

I suppose I'd always wanted to be famous. It's the same for everyone. If you're not famous, you don't exist. I wasn't actually going to write the book myself; it was being written by a ghost writer – someone who'd worked with a number of celebrities. But the publishing company said that I had to pretend I was writing the book myself, and that it might be difficult if I were asked any questions regarding the writing process. They gave me some examples of the type of difficult questions I might be asked – like: 'Do you write during the day, or at night?'; 'How many words a day do you write?'; 'Do you use a computer, or do you write the old-fashioned way with a pen or maybe a typewriter?'

Every two or three days I would receive an envelope by special delivery. Sometimes there would be nothing for a week and then two or three envelopes would arrive in the same day. Sometimes I'd get an envelope everyday for a week, and then nothing for two or three weeks. I'd been told that the ghost writer was in his seventies and that he refused to use a computer. His questions were typed out on a single sheet of yellow paper using a typewriter that printed some letters slightly higher than others. I had no idea why he chose to use yellow sheets of paper. Perhaps he had some kind of problem with his eyes – a congenital medical condition.

I tried to answer each of the questions as well as I could. On a few occasions I made something up, otherwise I would have to send the envelope back with nothing written on the sheet of yellow paper beneath the typed question. I didn't know the name of the school Joy had gone to, or the street she'd grown up on, or what profession she'd wanted to follow as a child. I didn't know the names of her grandparents or any of her aunts and uncles and cousins. I was relieved to be able to supply at least the name of her son, even if I couldn't describe him beyond the photograph Joy had shown me of him sitting with his grandparents in their small wooden hut in northern Thailand.

I tried to explain myself a little by writing that things had been naturally difficult for me and that I'd probably forced myself to forget a lot of what had happened. I didn't know whether the ghost writer appreciated this kind of information or not. The contents of the next envelope to arrive made no reference either to the contents of the previous envelope or to the answers I'd returned. Sometimes I was convinced that I'd been sent the wrong envelope, and that perhaps the ghost writer was working on two autobiographies at the same time. For example, on one occasion I was asked at what age I'd learned to make crème brûlé; and on another whether I'd ever slept on a bunk bed in a static caravan.

The book was completed within two months and had been scheduled to be released for sale at the conclusion of Sebastien Bluot's trial. That way the publishers would be able to attract a certain amount of attention. Of course, the writing was execrable. I could have done better myself. I'd already emailed the publishing company with my concerns. They tried to reassure me, saying that it was perfectly natural to get a little nervous and to have a few doubts so close to publication, but that the book was expected to sell well and so I had to be confident and to trust their professional judgment.

Nevertheless, I'd started to write my own book; perhaps as an antidote to the poison the ghost-writer had caused me to consume. I certainly wouldn't recommend reading a book you have supposedly written yourself about your dead, murdered wife. I have to admit that he captured some of the scenes of our life together quite well; particularly Joy's funeral and the parting moment of our marriage as I stood alone outside the little chapel in Leuven. But reading the thing brought back my insomnia, and when I did finally manage to fall off to sleep, under the influence of four or five sleeping tablets and an increased dosage of my medication, my nightmares were unbearably horrible, full of murder and incest and sodomy.

Perhaps writing was a form of self-medication. I began to spend every afternoon in the villa working on my own book about Joy, sitting in the battered wicker armchair in the small empty bedroom. I was certainly intending to call my book *Joy*, even if I'd supposedly already written a book by that title – even if I didn't know much about her life. Joy had by far the more interesting story to tell. But I soon realised that I wasn't in a position to write about her life as though I were seeing it through her eyes. I would be lying if I said I knew what she was thinking at any particular moment.

Perhaps I could quote something from the ghost writer's book. He names the school that she went to, despite my inability to help on the subject, and describes the appalling conditions inside a factory where she worked at the age of sixteen. I don't know how he found out about these things. As far as I'm aware, he hadn't travelled to Thailand.

One of the most moving chapters in the book describes Joy waving goodbye to her son at the bus station, and her first night alone in Bangkok. As the bus pulls away from the kerb, Joy presses the palm of her hand to the glass and smiles at her son. He's waving at her, his wrist and elbow jerking enthusiastically in the air, his lips mouthing the words she can't hear over and over again: 'Bye Mum'.

It was horrible to think of Joy being forced to leave her young son with his grandparents, perhaps for months or even years, so that she could find work in the city; but it was far from unusual for peasants in the countryside. On the journey to Bangkok, Joy seems to have been in a relatively good mood. The ghost writer goes on to describe her making friends with a passenger on the coach, a young woman travelling to Bangkok for similar reasons to her own. Her new friend was as attractive and intelligent as Joy and they soon decided to share a room and to look for work in a karaoke bar.

I had the impression that the ghost writer didn't wish to be associated with the book. None of the emails from the publishing company ever seemed to refer to him directly. Even when he'd written to me personally on his yellow paper there hadn't been a name preceding the address on the pre-paid envelope to which the sheet of yellow paper was to be returned.

He seemed to be a little reserved, considering the subject matter. There wasn't a single description of Joy's vagina, though it had been exceptionally beautiful even when measured by the cosmetically enhanced symmetrical minimalism of the porn industry. Perhaps the ghost writer was a little too old and the individuality of a particular vagina a little too difficult to describe. I still found myself thinking about Joy's vagina; sometimes her anus, too – but the images would start to fade before they'd had the chance to form into a coherent whole. Only her face remained unharmed inside my head, a flickering still protected from the destructive vagaries of my memory, neither happy nor sad.

27

M Y APPEARANCE ON the daytime chat show went relatively well. I made the dramatic announcement that I
was addicted to prescription painkillers three minutes into the
interview. The presenter seemed genuinely shocked. A camera
moved into position to get a close-up of her face. For a few
seconds she didn't know what to say. I thought that perhaps
someone was saying something in her earpiece. Perhaps she
was being told to act shocked for a little longer.

I'd waited a little too long to make the announcement. My
interview had been scheduled to last for three minutes and
thirty-five seconds. The presenter said that it must have been
terrible for me, living with this horrible secret. She looked sym-
pathetic. I said that it was a difficult situation and that I didn't
want to lie to anyone any more. The presenter said that I'd
been through a lot and that anyone would find losing a loved
one in that way very difficult to cope with. When I started to
cry she moved across to the lime-green sofa I was sitting on
and sat beside me with a box of tissues and her arm around my
shoulders. She smelled nice. She rubbed my back and gave me
a tissue and I could feel her left breast pressing into my side as
some of the cameras moved into new positions again.

I hadn't intended to start crying, but the television presenter
reacted to the situation with a calm professionalism. When I'd
been able to regain my composure, she said that we were going

to take a short break to give me a little time on my own, and that we would continue with the interview after the advertisements.

I was left sitting on the lime-green sofa and a woman wearing a pair of headphones asked me if I'd like a glass of water. I said that I didn't and the woman said that if I changed my mind she would go and get one for me. I looked out of the window at the blue sky and the clouds, at the leaves of the trees blowing in the wind. Of course, it wasn't a real window but a television screen playing a looped recording. The set had been built to resemble a living room so that the viewers felt as though they were part of a warm, loving family that had nice, interesting chats about things. In front of the window there was a vase of flowers placed on a small table. I hadn't watched the programme before so I didn't really know if the screen was playing a looped recording or not. The weather was the same as what I would have expected to see if I'd been looking out of a real window.

When the presenter returned and sat back in her position on the sofa opposite me, I thought about asking whether the screen was showing the actual view from a window somewhere in the building we were in, but before I had a chance she asked me if I was feeling well enough to continue with the interview. I said that I was feeling OK. She nodded and smiled again, before crossing something out in her script and writing something above whatever she'd crossed out. Lost for a second in thought, she scratched at a small patch of dry, chalky skin on her left knee. I looked at her hands and legs. Her fingernails were short and beautifully manicured, the light pink varnish glistening like a strawberry sorbet.

The programme's script had been printed on sheets of yellow paper like the kind the ghost writer used to type his questions on. I was wondering whether he'd worked on some kind of television programme when someone shouted the words 'back in ten seconds'. The television presenter looked up and smiled.

'Just relax and take your time, Raymond. You'll be fine.'

The same person who had shouted 'ten seconds' counted down from five to three. The television presenter turned her head a little to stare directly at a camera not far behind the sofa I was sitting on.

'Welcome back. Before the break we were discussing the book *The Life and Death of a Porn Star*, the biography of Joy Valentine, brutally murdered in 2010. I'm happy to say that the author of the book is still here with me.'

The television presenter turned to me and smiled. 'We don't wish to dwell on the subject; it is of course a private matter – but you said before the break that you are in fact addicted to prescription painkillers?'

'Yes. It's difficult for me to admit to something like that. It's been a secret for a long time. I haven't really told anyone.'

'It's strange, but sometimes a television programme is the easiest place to talk about things.'

I nodded my head. 'I suppose I just needed to tell someone.'

'We've helped a lot of people, Raymond. We'll give you all the support you need. Don't forget that you've done the hardest part now. You should be proud of yourself.'

'Thank you.'

The television presenter smiled warmly and tilted her head like a friendly, quizzical dog.

'Your book is really fascinating. It's such a sad story. But as you say, Joy was such a wonderful person and it's important to celebrate her life.'

'Yes. She was very special.'

'What did she think about Belgium?'

'She loved the snow. I think it snowed for two or three days during her first Christmas here.'

'That must be a really special memory for you.'

'Yes, it is.'

'Well, I urge everyone to buy your book. *Joy Valentine: The Life and Death of a Porn Star*. Thanks for coming in, Raymond.'

I nodded my head again and smiled. I could feel a camera moving behind me silently, a cool static playing against the hairs at the back of my neck. I tried my best not to move even though I wanted to look over my shoulder. Again the television presenter looked past me at a point somewhere beyond the sofa I was sitting on. As she started to speak about an item still to come on the programme, next season's fashion for authentic knitwear, the camera that had been pointing at me slid smoothly backwards across the floor and lowered its impenetrable black stare to something in a corner of the studio.

After seven or eight seconds, the woman with the clipboard motioned for me to walk quietly towards her. I glanced at the television presenter but she was looking at the machine that scrolled the words she had to say. I would never have imagined that it would be so nice to have a camera pointing at you, even though it had been a little disconcerting to begin with. I felt confident and important, as though my soul had been warmed with love.

The woman with the clipboard passed me over to another woman who led me along a series of corridors to a room with a sofa in it. I sat down and waited, even though I didn't know what I was waiting for. This time the sofa was a bright orange colour.

28

LITTLE CHERRY-COLOURED FLOWER buds had sprouted on the branches of the bonsai tree. The little tree's machinations were a mystery to me. It seemed to shed its leaves and the thinnest of its outermost branches almost at will. And now it had decided to flower – or at least it had been thinking about flowering before the morning's rain had blown in from the north.

I took some painkillers and returned to the wicker chair, staring out of the window for the rest of the afternoon. The rain fell in sporadic bursts that meandered across the sea, each downpour cloaking itself in a thickening grey blanket as it engulfed the coast.

I took some photographs as the light began to fade in the early evening and uploaded them on to my profile page on THAILOVELINKS.COM. I'd received a new friend request from a woman called Angelina in Phuket. She'd attached a picture of her vagina to the friend request. I sent a message thanking her for the photograph, and said that I thought her pussy looked beautiful. She replied with a smiley face and said that the rain in my photographs looked beautiful, too.

I looked back out of the window. The image of the Thai woman's vagina splayed itself across the surface of the dunes as my eyes followed the drifting rain blowing across the empty beach. She was as beautiful as Joy, and momentarily caused me to forget what Joy had looked like. I chased the contours of her face across the beach and dunes to the grey pool of sea water rippling in the rain by the perimeter wall, her dark eyes and strong cheekbones, the delicate lines of her mouth and nose, each fading from my grasp like disturbed ghosts.

It had happened before, but my memory was beginning to fail me more often. It was difficult enough for me to remember last week. I found it virtually impossible to distinguish between the hundreds of visits I'd made to the supermarket. The various seasonal promotions advertised from brightly coloured signs hanging over the aisles seemed to change from week to week. When I'd been forced to sign a form at the bank, the date I'd written at the side of my signature had been wrong by two months. I'd asked for the date prior to signing, and the woman behind the customer service desk had presumed I'd only needed to know the day of the month, and not the actual month itself. In the end I chose to make an educated guess, based to some extent on a colourful summer dress worn by a young woman standing in the queue behind me. But it hadn't been July; and it hadn't occurred to me that summer fashions line the rails in women's clothes shops from early spring.

After it had gone dark I heated a meal-for-one in the microwave and emailed Angelina again. She'd clearly employed the services of a cosmetic surgeon to tidy up her vagina a little. I told her that I'd been thinking about having a penis extension and that it would be possible to gain an extra two or three inches when erect. But of course there were risks: my erections would necessarily change because the ligaments anchoring the muscles of the penis to the pelvis were released during the procedure. I had no idea how this would affect penetration, but the benefits certainly outweighed the risks. Perhaps soon it would be possible for cosmetic surgeons to grow big penises on the backs of laboratory rats. But as for the female genitalia – it was simply a matter of trimming the labia with a scalpel and tightening the walls of the vagina with excisions and stitches.

Angelina was probably a bar girl. There was a small possibility that she'd been able to afford cosmetic surgery through other means. The daughters of relatively wealthy businessmen would occasionally subscribe to THAILOVELINKS.COM in the hope of finding a boyfriend in London or New York. When I told her that I was from Belgium she said that she didn't know where Belgium was. I replied that the film *In Bruges*, starring Colin Farrell, had been filmed in the Belgian city of Bruges. Of course, Jean-Claude Van Damme had been born in Belgium, too.

For some reason I decided to log on to my Facebook account. I hadn't looked at my Facebook page for over a year. A woman who used to sit four desks away from me had uploaded some photographs of her child's first birthday. Her surname had changed, too, so I presumed that she'd been married. When I'd worked at Siemens she'd been having difficulties finding a boyfriend. She had a strange, irritating voice and it was virtually impossible not to hear her complaining. But beyond that I didn't know anything about her. I'd never bothered to have a conversation with her.

Before I logged off I checked my friend requests. I'd received 588, all of them since my appearance on television. There was a message from Agnes, too. I looked at her profile picture, a photograph of her on holiday, and clicked on the 'read' button. The message had been sent months earlier and asked whether I was coping with everything.

I turned my laptop off and ate my meal-for-one watching television. There was a programme about the history of cycling, and another about an estate agents in Liège. I watched some of the programme about cycling, before finally deciding on the documentary about the estate agents in Liège. In a quiet moment, Cédric, one of the estate agents, admitted that he hated Dutch speakers because they thought that all French speakers were lazy. But French speakers, he said, were generally friendly and polite and didn't try to mess you around. Besides, the Dutch are too much like the Germans. One of his colleagues laughed and called him a racist. Cédric replied that it had nothing to do with the colour of anyone's skin, it was just his opinion about things.

'I don't even consider myself a Belgian,' he said. 'It means nothing to me. We should be separate countries.'

His friend disagreed and said that Belgium was already too small, that it's better to be a big country than a small country, just as it's better to be a big man than a small man. No one wants to be a small man.

I finished my meal-for-one and stared at the black patch of sky visible through the window. The weather must have cleared a little because I could see some stars, even with the television on and the light from the screen lighting up the walls and the ceiling. Cédric was worrying about nothing. Like the villa I was living in, sooner or later Belgium itself was certain to be destroyed or annexed. Towards the end of the programme, the camera followed him to a bar in the centre of Liège before he made the journey to his apartment in the suburbs. He drank alone, occasionally saying something for the benefit of the camera. The enthusiasm he'd shown in the office had gone. He stared at the floor, his eyes glazed and empty, finally confiding that his own apartment was rather small and a little dirty.

'My neighbours are terrible and the entire building has a problem with mould on the walls. I've been trying to find somewhere else.'

Back at his apartment, Cédric self-consciously removed a

duvet and pillow from the sofa and took them to the bedroom, explaining that he'd taken to sleeping in the living room because he liked to fall asleep in front of the television. In a corner of the room, a pile of clothes lay abandoned on the floor in front of a collection of DVDs stacked against the wall.

I took two more painkillers and changed channels back to the programme about the history of cycling. An old man wearing gold-rimmed spectacles was being interviewed in his living room. Some medals and trophies were arranged on the shelves of a cabinet behind his armchair, together with a small collection of ornaments and family photographs. He'd won the Tour of Flanders in the 1950s as well as a bronze medal at the Olympic games.

29

I WOKE AT four in the afternoon and stood at the window. The sky had cleared and the sand dunes had dried in the sun. More clouds were coming in from the north and the sea was beginning to darken.

Some of the bonsai tree's flower buds had opened, each a ruffle of pink smaller than an infant's fingernail. I felt the moss growing across the twisted roots and added a drop of water from the small brass watering can. The flowers were pretty, like miniature roses clasping the velvet yellow dot of a stamen in the heart of their petals.

I sat in the wicker chair and stared at the bonsai tree, at the carpet of green moss and the umbrella of pink petals, at the tree's roots grasping like wizened fingers at a careful assemblage of stones that perfectly resembled a mountain rock face exposed by wind and rain.

The sound of a gull calling above the villa raised my eyes to the rotting window frame where the paint was peeling from the silvery wood. A dozen or so large gulls, blown in from the sea, circled in the air above the villa before landing out of sight somewhere on the roof. I looked at the flakes of paint curling from the surface of the windowsill and listened to the muffled sound of the birds' calls a few feet above my head. The occasional human word seemed almost discernible amidst the cackle of their caws and squabbles, broken sentences lost in the wind. I thought that I could hear the birds saying my name, my ears hanging on the silence as though they were about to augur in the staccato poetry of witches.

After a few minutes the gulls quietened down. I thought about going into the other room to turn on the television. I looked at the floorboards, at the path to the door worn into the wood. The smallest of efforts seemed virtually impossible. The muscles in my legs and arms had atrophied. Each time I went to the massage parlour it was a surprise to see in one of their large mirrors how thin my body had become. My ribs were visible, and my hips protruded horribly on either side of a mass of thick black hair. As the subcutaneous layer of fat above my pubis wasted away, my erections seemed bigger, my penis thicker and darker, obscene in its greed amidst the pale white of my thighs.

For the next hour I tried to convince myself to get up and to go to the bathroom to urinate. The dark mass of clouds was nearing the beach and I'd decided that I didn't want to miss the rain. Beyond, the sky had lightened to a greying yellow. The rain might pass in less than a minute.

My fingers moved obsessively backwards and forwards over the curving weave of the wicker chair's armrests. Close to the slowing reach of the waves, a huddle of small brown birds darted this way and that, their legs a blur of movement as they scattered in every direction before coming back together at the edge of the water. I'd seen them before. They were probably feeding, waiting for the waves to sieve invertebrates on to the beach. But of course I didn't know. They could have been playing a game to amuse themselves, or fighting to the death over territory and females.

I was probably considered as something of a regular at the massage parlour, even though I rarely spoke and never made an effort to start a conversation. I couldn't remember once giving my name to any of the girls. I hadn't had a conversation with anyone since appearing on the daytime chat show on television, if such a thing could be considered a conversation. Occasionally I talked to myself as I sat in the wicker chair or wandered around the villa, but days could pass in silence. My favourite television programmes had become my only form of company in the evenings. Perhaps it had been like that for a long time.

PART THREE

30

THE BODY OF a young woman has been found in the dunes by a man walking his dog. I was woken by the police knocking at the door. The detectives that came to question me didn't seem to suspect me of anything. After some general questions relating to whether I'd seen or heard anything unusual in the last three days, whether I'd witnessed any unusual behaviour or anything out of the ordinary, the two detectives thanked me for my cooperation and left.

The young woman's body has been covered by the kind of white tent you see on the news on television. The police forensics team are busy taking photographs and searching for evidence. Occasionally someone wearing a hooded white suit appears at the door of the tent. If I stand to the right side of the window in the bedroom where the bonsai tree sits on the windowsill, I can see them removing their masks to take a breath of fresh air and to talk for a minute with one of their colleagues.

I've spent all day digging out the perimeter wall. It's seven o'clock in the evening and I'm tired. I sit in the sand and look at the pale blue sky and the sea. The sand is cool beneath my hands. I don't get blisters any more. My palms are calloused and the skin feels thick and strong.

I saw a boat earlier today. It came close to the shore and

disappeared behind the dunes, too far away to see anyone onboard. I look out at the horizon, at the darkening grey water. My shirt is wet with sweat and the cotton is cold when it blows against my back in the wind. I can taste salt when I lick my lips and my forehead and cheeks feel gritty from dried sweat. Before I go inside to wash and eat, I look at the mounds of sand I've moved. Tomorrow I'll have to start all over again.

I stand up and steady myself on the slope of the dune. When I bend down to pick up my spade I realise how tired my muscles are. I have to use the spade like a walking stick to stop myself from falling over. I carry the spade up into my bedroom and lean it against the wall. I like looking at the dull polish the sand has brought to the metal and the greying smears of dirt left by my hands on the wooden handle.

I wash myself in the sink with cold water and heat a meal in the microwave. After I've eaten I sit in the wicker chair and look out of the window. Yesterday a young boy appeared from nowhere while I was digging out the perimeter wall. He sat on the top of a dune and watched me. I thought that he might have come to watch me again today. When I went for a drink of water he followed me into the villa and stood at the door while I filled a cup at the tap. I offered him a drink and he shook his head. When I told him that he shouldn't have followed me into the villa, he disappeared.

Some of his older friends had probably sent him to take a look inside the villa. A few nights ago a window was broken in the room containing my father's boxes. I'm probably suspected of the woman's murder. If anyone breaks into the villa, I'll split their head open with the spade.

I haven't written anything about the small bedroom full from floor to ceiling with the cardboard boxes that contain my father's belongings. Some of the larger boxes hold only a single object carefully wrapped in layered sheets of newspaper held together with yellowing tape that has become brittle and useless. Other boxes contain smaller boxes – some, like matryoshka dolls, hiding still smaller boxes inside them. They take up so much of the room that the window has been completely blocked and the light bulb obscured. Weak, angular slats of light illuminate the dust raised by my intrusions. There's barely enough space to edge from one side of the room to the other. I've taken to standing in the middle of the room, as far as the available floor space will allow, listening to the muffled silence before choosing a box to open more or less at random.

The ghost writer's book hasn't sold very well and I've been lucky that my father had developed a taste for Chinese porcelain: the sums being offered for even an average piece are exceptionally inflated. One of the pots I found sold at auction for nearly a thousand euros – a little vase I can't remember beyond its colour and that it was bought by a businessman living two hundred miles from Beijing.

I discovered through a book found in one of the boxes that the bonsai tree is in fact a *penjing* tree. The Japanese art originated from the much older Chinese, and the pot my father's tree is growing from was made in China over four hundred years ago. My father had collected all kinds of objects when I was a child. I can remember a small Japanese table that he would sit at crosslegged drinking tea; a large black Javanese wardrobe that gave me nightmares; a bulbous yellow lute hanging from the living room wall; and a brass Arabic water pipe for smoking hashish, and on which I'd tried to smoke everything from tea leaves and nettles to banana rind and paracetamol tablets.

I haven't yet found in the boxes I've opened any of the things I can remember from my childhood. Most of them contain faded old clothing and worn shoes; crockery and bed linen; broken household appliances.

Now that the window is broken in the room the air feels cool and fresh. I can hear the wind and the occasional gull as I sit behind the door and run my fingers around the crumpled corners of one of the boxes. Sometimes a certain box will intrigue me for no particular reason. This time I want to look inside a box that has half-collapsed under the weight of two other boxes placed on top of it. But perhaps I should open one of the heavier boxes. I think about it and look at them. After a few minutes I decide to stick with the box that first caught my attention. I lift the two heavier boxes off the collapsed box and sit back down to open it. I run my finger underneath the lid at the sides of each flap and the brittle tape breaks. Then I force my finger through the tape joining each flap at the centre and open the cardboard lid.

Inside, I find one half of a pair of flowered cream curtains. A lamp with a flattened lampshade. A rough felt blanket. A tin of house paint. A rear bicycle light. A small leather case containing shoe polish and brushes. A washing up bowl encrusted with dirt. I don't understand why the boxes have been packed so ridiculously, as though someone had been forced to clear away the remains of a jumble sale in a hurry. If the young boy comes back I'll ask him if he'd like to make a fire in the garden and help me burn some of my father's things. It would be a good idea to make friends with him. I don't want his acquaintances breaking any more of my windows.

3 1

A STRANGE GREEN insect has found its way across the windowsill to the bonsai tree. I've been watching it for three hours. If I lean close enough I can see that its body is translucent and that it resembles a locust, though it's smaller than an ant and doesn't have wings. Three of its inner organs are visible: one black, one brown and one a pale yellow. Perhaps it's hoping to eat the little tree's leaves.

I dug out the perimeter wall until I was hungry and then I came inside for something to eat. I had a little too much to drink last night and my muscles are aching. I light another cigarette and think about making a cup of coffee. The insect finds its way up on to the rim of the bowl the bonsai tree sits in. It circles, clockwise, and then stops. The villa seems to attract a lot of insects. Yesterday a butterfly flew twice through the window, each time fluttering around for a matter of seconds before leaving. And yet a bluebottle will irritate me for hours, unable to escape, until I have to get up and kill the thing.

I open the window to listen to the wind and the sea. Sometimes the pools of warm stagnant water smell of muddy, rotten fish and the stench blows up into the room. At other times the air is cool and fresh: marram grass, sea buckthorn, pine – a pale, northern maquis.

When I stand up to leave the room my thighs ache with the effort. If I make another cup of coffee I won't want to go back outside to finish the rest of the afternoon's digging. I drink a cup of water in the bathroom and pick up my spade, using it as a walking stick to help me downstairs. After a few minutes of digging I'll be fine. I've moved around to the western side of the perimeter wall and the sun will warm my muscles. I tell myself that I shouldn't drink so much, that my legs are stiff because I drank two bottles of wine last night.

The first few spades are difficult and I curse myself until I see the boy watching me from the top of a dune. I dreamed that I asked him if he'd like to live in the villa with me and he told me that he couldn't leave his mother. I came to understand that his mother was Joy, that she wasn't dead after all, though the woman he brought to the villa looked only occasionally like her.

I dig the spade into the sloping sand and try to catch my breath. The boy is still watching me from the dune. I look up at him. He's sitting with his chin lowered to his chest, his right hand pulling up tufts of marram grass and throwing them into the air above his bare feet.

I pull the spade from the sand and move into a position where I won't have my back to the boy. I'm not wearing shoes either. It's easier to walk in the deep sand when you aren't wearing shoes. Perhaps the boy is on holiday and his mother has left him to play on the beach.

I continue digging, shovelling the sand from the side of a small dune until it collapses. The boy seems fascinated by what I'm doing. He stops pulling up the marram grass by the roots and raises his head to look over the perimeter wall at the villa.

I look up at him.

'I had a dream about your mother last night.'

The boy pulls a face, narrowing his eyes.

'She came to live in the villa with me.'

He thinks about it for a moment. 'In your house?'

'Yes. In my house.'

He raises his head and looks over the perimeter wall at the villa, as though he expects to see his mother standing at a window.

'Why did she come and live with you?'

'We were in love.'

The boy grabs a handful of sand from between his legs, letting it fall through his fingers on to the top of his knee before patting it flat with the palm of his hand. I turn and continue shovelling the sand away from the perimeter wall. After a few minutes the boy leaves and I walk to the top of the dune to see where he's gone. He's running across the beach towards the path. I go back to my spade and look at the grey sky, at the distant pine trees beyond the villa. The sand is getting wet and heavy as I get deeper. It slides from the spade in rectangular lumps. It's easier to dig like that, even though it takes more of an effort. The small dune of sand piled against the perimeter wall soon starts to disappear. When the sun sets I go inside exhausted and make something to eat.

3 2

I'VE SEEN A tall woman walking along the beach this morning, her head and shoulders wrapped in a shawl against the bad weather. I wondered whether she'd come to take a look at the villa; whether the boy had told his mother about me. She stood staring out to sea and turned to glance over her shoulder through the rain. I was sitting watching her. When it's raining I like more than ever to sit at the window. The frayed wicker chair is surprisingly comfortable. After a few minutes the woman retraced the line of footprints she'd left in the sand and disappeared behind one of the dunes to the right of my window.

It takes the rain a long time to wash away the woman's footprints. In an undulation in the beach her feet have left little craters that have now filled with pools of water. I watch the raised hollow circles slowly melt to nothing over the course of the afternoon.

A powdery beige moth has replaced the colourful butterfly that flew into the room. I caught it in my hand and then decided to let it go. It sits on the wall less than a few feet from a large knotted cobweb hanging from the ceiling. Occasionally it flies about erratically before landing in more or less the same position. The cobweb has been abandoned and is now only a heavy tangle of grey dust.

When the woman's footprints have disappeared I go down

to the garage. The water level has risen a little. I can only stand on the seventh step down from the door. Yesterday I counted eight. The water has reached halfway up the chrome wing-mirror on my father's car. A scum of detritus floats against the windows, the surface of the water as still as black glass.

Perhaps the rising damp has affected the electronics inside the television. Last night a blue colouration appeared on a part of the screen, blurring the left side of the newsreader's face. It mirrored the distorting of my own face – a bruised swelling that has become infected in the right side of my jaw. I vaguely remember falling and banging my head. Some of my teeth feel loose and there is a large gash inside my mouth. There isn't a mirror in the villa and I can only catch vague glimpses of myself in the windows. Even with dirty hands I find it hard to keep myself from touching the weeping green hole of flesh inside my cheek. The pain caused by picking at the wound has an element of pleasure to it. It reminded me of my mother and the strange habit she used to have. Every evening she would sit in her armchair incessantly scratching her legs until they bled – a side-effect of the obscure medications I would hear her taking at her bedroom sink – her brightly painted finger-nails diligently removing the brown, scaly lids from sores that were never allowed to heal, one after the other as she watched television. She seemed to enjoy it and collected the remains in a tissue she would fold and conceal in the sleeve of her blouse or cardigan. It took up her time as knitting might have done and her skin was cratered with small, weeping sores from her knees to her ankles.

I leave the garage and go up to the room containing my father's boxes. I don't know how many I've yet to look through. After I've finished with one I put it back where I found it. I still like to stand in the middle of the room, but the silence has gone because of the broken window. I edge through the middle of the room as far as the available floor space will allow. After a few minutes I choose a box more or less at random, a small one covered with shards of broken glass.

I like breaking the tape with my fingers. Sometimes the tape hasn't turned brittle and I can't manage to push a hole through it. When that happens I rip the box open from the side. I find a weakened point on the box I've chosen and test the tape's strength with my finger. My nail pushes through with a satisfying, almost imperceptible crackle, and I run it down the middle of the lid and then along the sides, separating the two flaps.

The contents have been covered with an old newspaper. I take it out and look at the front page. The story is uninteresting and I don't bother to read anything more than a few words. In the box I find an ornament that I remember sitting on top of the gas fire in my father's dining room. For some reason it reminds me of my mother again, even though she never lived in that particular house. He moved into the house with the gas fire in the dining room after he'd left the house my mother and I lived in. I hold the ornament in my hands and look at it. It's ugly and garishly coloured – a weasel perching on a rotten apple.

I leave the rest of the contents undiscovered inside the box and go into the small bedroom to sit in the wicker chair. It's still raining and the weather has closed in. I can barely see the beach through the grey mist.

The publishing company has decided that it doesn't wish to express an interest in my book, to use the common vernacular. Nevertheless, occasionally I continue to write something. I'd been hoping to write a certain amount of words each day, but it's been virtually impossible. I have to dig out the perimeter wall and in the evenings I'm too tired to think. Nothing comes easily, and whatever I write is usually deleted a day or so later.

A few days ago I found my copy of the ghostwriter's book

buried under a pile of my things. I flick through the pages to the photographs of Joy. None of the photographs are pornographic; in one she can be seen half-naked, but with her breasts covered by her arms and elbows. The rest are photographs of her in Thailand, or smiling with the friends she'd made in Belgium.

I still occasionally receive a cheque from the publishers. The post office has decided that my address is inaccessible and that any letters sent to me will be held at their collections office. Sometimes the cheques aren't enough to warrant the walk from the collections office to the bank. I imagine bumping into the ghost writer in the queue at the counter, both of us with our little cheques in our hands.

I turn the pages of the ghost writer's book and read half of a paragraph, something about Joy's last day. She spoke to a friend on the phone and looked on the internet at holidays in Italy before walking to the supermarket on Parijsstraat. I don't know where Parijsstraat is. I never really bothered to learn the names of the streets around my apartment. Perhaps it was the Carrefour Express on the corner. Personally, I never liked the Carrefour Express. I preferred the Carrefour Market if I wanted to go to a Carrefour. Everyone is in a rush to purchase perhaps two or three items in the Carrefour Express. You're not invited to take your time, to wander at leisure amongst the aisles. And besides, they don't have a good selection of microwave meals.

33

I'VE BEEN ASKED for my mobile phone number by Kimberley, a beautiful young woman who is my friend on THAILOVELINKS.COM. I'm thinking about sending a text message to her but I can't think what to write. She describes herself on her profile page as an amateur photographer and she's uploaded some photographs she took for a college project. She left a comment saying that she really liked my photographs and I left a comment saying that I really liked her photographs, too. A few of my friends have commented on the photos I've taken of the beach and the dunes, but none of them have ever asked for my phone number before. I'm not really sure why Kimberley has asked for my phone number.

My mobile phone has been lying untouched on the bedroom floor for months. Every so often I'll make an effort to look for it amongst the detritus of dirty clothes and half-eaten microwave meals, and when I've satisfied myself that no one has bothered to send a text message to me, I'll plug it into its charger until I hear the bleep that tells me the battery is full.

Perhaps I could ask Kimberley what the weather has been like, or whether she enjoyed her day. I don't know much about her. On her profile page she describes herself as loving photography more than anything in the world. But she's only used the one sentence and the rest of the allotted space has been left blank. Her height is five feet eight inches and she is a slim, attractive non-smoker and social drinker. At least she's made the effort to tick the 'likes art and museums' box, the 'likes going to the cinema' box, and the 'looking to have fun' box.

I click the new message button on my mobile phone and start the first words of a text message, before giving up and deleting what I've written.

I stare at the blank screen. I'm sitting on the floor against the wall in the small bedroom. The bare floorboards feel relatively warm under my left hand. I move a little and the wall behind my back feels cold. I look up at the ceiling. The white paint has turned a light shade of darkening grey where the ceiling meets the wall. I put my mobile phone down and push my hand against the nearest box to see how heavy it is. It's one of the largest boxes and I can't manage to move it while I'm sitting down. I've probably tried to move it before in exactly the same manner.

I wonder what could be so heavy and then pick up my mobile phone and look at the screen again. After a few minutes I send a text message to Kimberley asking if it's alright for me to send a text message to her. I almost press the cancel button while the message is being delivered. I couldn't think of anything else to write. But about thirty seconds later she replies. She says that she's watching television and that she's bored. I don't know what to respond with. I think about telling her that I'm staring at the wall, but in the end I tell her that I'm sitting looking out of the window at the sea and that it looks really beautiful.

Kimberley asks me to take a photograph and to send it to her mobile phone. I get up and go into the other room and sit in the wicker chair. The window is dirty and the windowsill is covered with dust. I focus on the beach and the waves and press the capture button. The dirty window and the mould growing between the glass and the wooden window frame are just a blur in the foreground. When I send the photograph to Kimberley she replies that the sea looks very cold. I say that I don't know how cold it is and that I've never tried to swim in it.

Kimberley seems to really like texting with me. I almost think about calling her, but I know that it's probably too soon. If anything, it's better just to send a text message. It seems easier that way.

I look at my reflection in the window.

'Hi Kimberley.'

'I just thought I'd give you a call.'

My voice sounds strange because the inside of my mouth is swollen.

'I just thought I'd give you a call . . .'

'Hi.'

'I was hoping you'd call me.'

'I didn't really want to ask.'

'My voice sounds a little strange because . . .'

'. . . I have an infection inside my mouth.'

'But it's nothing serious...'

'. . . There's nothing seriously wrong with me.'

I open my mouth wide and stare at my reflection. My tongue and throat seem to be floating over the beach as I raise my head and twist my neck. Moving my jaw and stretching my lips across my teeth causes the wound to open again. Blood stains my tongue and looks grey in the glass.

'There's nothing seriously wrong with me.'

'. . . Thanks for calling.'

'I'm really glad you called.'

'It's nice to hear your voice.'

'We should talk more often.'

'Thank you. I would like that.'

34

In the end I don't bother to call Kimberley. For some reason she has searched for my name on the internet. Perhaps she wanted to check that I hadn't murdered anyone.

She says that she's been reading about Joy and that it's terrible what has happened to her. Since I haven't told her about Joy, she could only have found out by searching for my name on the internet.

I think about deleting her from my list of friends. She'll probably delete me. At the moment, she'll hesitate because she doesn't want me to think she's cruel, or because she doesn't want to hurt my feelings too much. But in a few days, hoping that I won't notice, she'll click on the 'remove from friends' button. No woman wants to associate with a man whose wife has been brutally murdered.

I take a look at her profile page again. Nothing's changed. Her photos are the same and she hasn't written anything in the box where you're supposed to describe yourself. There's just the one sentence: 'I love photography more than anything in the world.'

I turn my laptop off for the first time in a week and take some painkillers. The swelling in my mouth is getting worse. The pain has spread from my jaw into my ear and the back of my skull. I went to bed at four in the morning and lay awake listening to a fly buzzing around the room until two in the afternoon. I've taken a full box of tablets and nothing has happened. Occasionally the fly appears from somewhere and lands on the same dirty plate on the floor to crawl around the rotting remains of a microwave meal.

The television's health is deteriorating too. The discoloration has spread across the screen, a nauseous liquid infection of blue and pink, yellowing and green at its furthest edge. The afternoon programme on La Une makes virtually no sense to me. A series of guests are introduced and they each talk about something in particular. I vaguely recognise the face of a dark-haired woman nervously stroking her pale throat, her chin raised as though in defence against an accusation. Her left eye and cheek have been bruised by the blue and pink of the television screen. The programme cuts to a scene from a film and the woman is standing with her back to the wall in the shadows of a dark street. It's raining and the woman's hair has blackened in the downpour. A man in a raincoat is looking for her. The woman steps out from the shadows and raises a gun, shooting the man as he turns to face her in the dim yellow streetlight.

I mute the volume with the remote control and listen as the hiss of static fades to silence. I thought I could hear someone knocking at the front door. A dune has almost buried the two-metre-high gate and it would be easy for someone to step over what remains. I think about turning the television off in case whoever it is can see the light from the screen reflected in the window. I slowly raise my arm and move my thumb to the red button on the remote control. Someone knocks again, louder than before and perhaps a little aggressively. I press the red button on the remote control and the television screen fades to black. I don't move except to lower my arm on to the mattress by my side.

I can hear a faint breeze blowing against the window and

the calling of a bird in the sky above the villa. After a minute or so whoever has climbed over the gate knocks at the door again. They're probably from an electricity company. They'll want to know if I've considered changing from my current electricity supplier and I won't know what to say.

They knock again, louder, as though they're irritated that I haven't answered the door. It seems pointless to try and ignore them. Perhaps it's the police. A body could have been found on the dunes. I get up and go downstairs. I haven't changed my T-shirt for weeks and it's stained with the remains of the food I've spilt whilst eating in bed. I notice that the crotch of my pyjama trousers is stained, too, with what looks like dried, flaking patches of semen. It's only when you're faced with a certain objectivity that you notice these things.

As I open the door I remember that I can't speak very well because of the swelling in my mouth. Anyway, I don't try to hide my irritation and my words sound more like a mumbled growl.

'I was trying to sleep. I'm not very well.'

'I'm sorry to disturb you. Especially on a lovely day like today.'

A young electricity company employee smiles and tries to ignore my swollen face and the dirty T-shirt and pyjama trousers I'm wearing. I find myself staring at him as he begins to make his speech, my eyes half closed as I balance myself against the door frame. His skin is a little orange and he's wearing a pair of pointed shoes.

I nod my head, but the pain in my mouth causes me to wince and close my eyes. When I open them again the man from the electricity company has stopped talking.

'I'm sorry. I have an infection inside my mouth. Would you like to come in?'

I step aside and raise my hand a little as an invitation. The man from the electricity company hesitates. I don't know if he's understood me.

'I haven't spoken to a human being for a long time.'

I can smell the strong combination of aftershave and deodorant that the electricity company employee is wearing. Perhaps it will mask the smell of my own body. The variety of odours that my body is capable of producing is really astounding. I suppose I find them fascinating. As I walk into the living room I think about apologising. The living room is disgusting too. The floor is covered with rubbish and there's only one chair.

'I'm sorry about the way I smell,' I say as though commenting on some minor triviality in order to progress a necessary conversation between strangers. 'I don't get many visitors, so there doesn't seem much point in washing. When I go to the supermarket, I usually try and make something of an effort.'

The electricity company employee attempts to smile politely. For some reason we are standing very close to the wall opposite the door inside the living room.

I point and nod towards the armchair. 'Please, sit down. There's only one chair.'

'I'm fine. Really . . .'

'No, please. I can stand over there and we can talk like that.'

I go over to the wall by the sliding doors and the electricity company employee sits on the edge of the armchair with his clipboard balancing on his knees. The armchair is still facing the corner of the room where the television used to be and so he has to twist his body a little and turn his head in my direction.

'So as I was saying, our sustainability ambitions are at the heart of a continuing commitment to environmental . . .'

I turn and look out through the sliding doors at the dunes and the rectangle of sand inside the perimeter wall.

'The problem is that I don't feel very well.'

The electricity company employee looks up at me. 'Would you like me to come back tomorrow?'

'I don't think I'll be better tomorrow.'

'How about Thursday?'

'I'll probably need to think about it.'

I push myself away from the sliding doors and stand in the middle of the room, swaying a little in a slow, circular movement of my head and shoulders.

'Could we talk about something else perhaps?'

I look at him and open my mouth, pulling my jaw down with my fingers to ease the pain.

'I can see that you're in some discomfort, Mr Verleaux.'

The man from the electricity company stands up and waits for me to move out of the way so he can walk to the front door. I lower my head and stuff my fingers further into my mouth, raising my elbow and prising my thumb between my cheek and jaw.

'I'll schedule Thursday with the appointments team . . .'

I take my fingers out of my mouth and look at him suspiciously.

'How do you know my name?'

'Excuse me?'

'How do you know my name? You just used my name, and I want to know how you know what my name is?'

'Your information has been stored on our database.'

'No. You're lying,' I shout, clenching my fists. 'You've been sent by a magazine.'

'I haven't been sent by a magazine. I told you where I was from.'

'You think I killed my wife, don't you?'

He doesn't say anything and I wonder whether he can understand what I'm saying. As he steps outside and walks across the sand to what remains of the buried gate I start to wonder if he's been taking photographs inside the villa. I shout at him as he's struggling to climb up the side of the dune that's blown over the perimeter wall. He stops and looks over his shoulder, his hands and feet buried in the sand. When he reaches the top of the dune I go upstairs and watch him from the bedroom window. He seems to know that I'm watching him even though he doesn't look at the villa when he glances over his shoulder to see if he's being followed.

I lie down on the mattress and stare at the ceiling before turning the television back on. Marie-Pierre Mouligneau is standing in a field of yellow tulips. She smiles at the camera and says that it isn't difficult to understand why these beautiful flowers are so popular.

35

O N MY BIRTHDAY I decide to take a look at my Facebook page. I'd been forcing myself to forget that it was my birthday. Or, rather, I'd been pretending to forget that it was my birthday. It seems virtually impossible to really forget something like that.

It takes me five attempts to remember my password and then I realise that the entire website has been completely redesigned. I stare at the screen for a few minutes. I have no messages and only two friend requests. Perhaps I'd been hoping for someone to have wished me a happy birthday.

Almost immediately, I see a photograph of my former manager at the bottom of the screen. I can't remember his name until I see it written next to his profile photograph. I didn't even know I was friends with him on Facebook. I consider looking at his profile page. Perhaps he and Agnes were married and they have children and a nice house. I don't know. I suppose I'm not very curious when it comes to things like that.

I stare at the computer screen. An advertisement appears featuring a pretty young woman in a short summer dress. The woman's dress blows up in a breeze as she's walking along a city street, momentarily revealing her panties before she has the time to grab at the dress's hem. I think about Agnes, and imagine her lifting her skirt to reveal her panties to me, the folds of her labia visible under a soft white satin. I've always been more or less obsessed with panties. You could almost believe they were more interesting than what lies beneath, every woman veiling herself in a magic cloak. I once found a pair on the street next to a car, and noticed that they were a little stained in the gusset as I slipped them into my pocket and took them home, my heart pounding in my chest as though I'd found a fragment of the Turin shroud.

I scroll through my friends and find Agnes. She looks older, with one or two nascent wrinkles developing around her eyes. The photograph of her has been taken by someone else, on a beach at sunset. It's enough to keep me from clicking on to her profile page.

I turn my laptop off. My birthday treat wasn't very inspiring. I don't know what I was expecting. At least I've made two new friends, even though I didn't bother to learn either of their names. I get up off the mattress and go into the small bedroom. Perhaps the contents of one of the few remaining unopened boxes could be a present to myself. There's one I've been keeping my eye on for months, waiting for the right moment, even though there's nothing particularly different about its appearance.

I tilt the box a little to feel its weight, and then drag it across the floor to the chair in the corner. The tape sealing the two halves of the lid breaks easily and I run my finger from edge to edge between the rectangles of cardboard. Inside, I find the usual jumble of useless household objects: half a dozen mantelpiece ornaments, an old transistor radio, a recipe book for the first-time buyer of a Braun food processor, a box of coloured lightbulbs, three small glasses with cartoon characters painted on their sides, a collection of cassette tapes with their sleeves missing. There doesn't seem to be anything even vaguely interesting in the box.

I close the lid and sit and listen to the air blowing through the broken window. I've managed to sort through enough boxes for a part of the window to become visible and I can see that it's raining. I listen to the rain falling on the roof and look at the branches of the trees blowing in the distance, a small moving blur of dark greens and reddish browns and the thin white trunks of a dozen silver birches. I usually try to make an effort on my birthday, even if it's just a walk to the supermarket to buy something for myself. I haven't been out of the villa for over a week.

I light a cigarette and go into the other bedroom and sit in the wicker chair, then stand up at the window and look at the sea. Further out, the waves have darkened to the colour of slate and coal. After I've finished my cigarette I put it out on the floor with my foot and light another. I've had to learn to smoke from the left side of my mouth. The infection seems to be getting neither better nor worse, it only changes a little in its varieties of pain and swelling.

The rain has started to drip through the hole in the ceiling. I look at where the dusty floorboards have been cleaned by falling water. The wood looks almost orange. I look up at the ceiling, at the hole in the crumbling plaster and the drops of water falling from a peeling flake of white paint. It takes five seconds for each drop to form and then fall to the floor. I count the seconds between each drop, and then turn back to the window and listen to them falling like the slow tick of a clock.

The bonsai tree's leaves have started to wither in the cold weather. I can't remember when I last watered its soil. The little brass watering can is empty on the floor. I pick it up and walk to the bathroom, turn the tap, stand at the sink while it fills, then go back into the small bedroom and pour some water into the bonsai tree's pot.

If it wasn't for the infection in my mouth I could have

gone to the massage parlour for my birthday. But my breath is disgusting and I don't want to humiliate myself by having to struggle to speak from behind my hand. I'm not sure the woman behind the reception desk would understand me anyway. When I talk aloud to myself I can only hear a barrage of glottal burbles muffled by my swollen tongue and cheek.

I open my mouth and think about saying something to the bonsai tree, but I can't think of anything to say, and in the end I don't bother. I'm not sure anyone has ever really talked to a house plant. A dog, or a cat, yes; maybe even a budgerigar or the television – but surely not an aspidistra ignored in a corner, a vase of carnations dying on the mantelpiece. . . ? Perhaps it takes a heartbeat, a pair of eyes, a nose and a mouth.

I stand up and walk around the room a little, pausing by the far wall opposite the window. The rain is beating against the glass and the clouds have closed in. I walk over to where the drip of water is falling from the ceiling and hold out my hand. A droplet lands on my wrist, wetting my veins and tendons. I move my hand a little until a droplet falls into my palm. I count four seconds. Another droplet lands in my palm. I look up at the ceiling and watch the water forming into a little bulb on the edge of the peeling flake of paint, moving my head quickly enough for my eyes to follow as it drops and falls through the air and into my hand.

I can hear the wind through the hole in the ceiling, the rain battering against the roof in gusts. I cup my hand and let the droplets collect in my palm until a clear pool spills through my fingers and runs down my arm. I raise my hand to my lips and empty what remains into my mouth. Most of the water runs down my chin and neck because I can't open my mouth very well, but the little bit I manage to drink tastes good, a little earthy, as though it had passed through a blanket of moss.

I light a cigarette and lean against the wall by the edge of the circle of wet floorboards. If I look through the window from here, I can see more of the beach than when I'm sitting in the wicker chair. But there isn't much to look at: a flat expanse of wet brown sand shrouded in rain and mist. I finish my cigarette and think about going for a walk to the supermarket to look for a birthday present for myself.

36

I LEAVE THE villa three days later and catch the bus to the Carrefour hypermarket to buy myself a birthday present.

It's late in the afternoon and the bus is full of noisy teenagers making their way home from school. I wipe the condensation from the window and press my cheek and jaw against the cold glass. I'm a little hung-over and I have a headache. I'd been considering going to the massage parlour but I don't think I'm going to bother. I look at the rows of houses and small gardens and the cars parked by the side of the road. Every thirty seconds one of the teenagers screams or shouts at the top of their voice. They remind me of the adolescent chimpanzees I've seen on wildlife programmes. When I look over my shoulder I see that one of them is even swinging from a hand rail. I calm myself down with the thought that if the bus were to crash he would probably be thrown through the window. Maybe he would get crushed under the wheels, too.

I'd mistakenly thought it might be nice to sit in the company of other human beings. I hadn't considered the possibility of children. But eventually, the bus arrives at the supermarket and circles the car park before coming to a stop not far from the entrance. Three old ladies shuffle off in front of me and I'm followed through the supermarket's electric doors by a goth – in particular an adult male goth. I wait by the shopping trolleys and allow him to overtake me. It's almost impossible not to look at the enormous black boots he's wearing, with four-inch-thick rubber soles and shiny metal toecaps and shin guards. Rather surprisingly he makes his way to the birthday cards aisle. Perhaps you would expect him to go straight to the knives and alcohol. For some reason it seems a little disconcerting to see a goth pushing a shopping trolley around a supermarket.

I take one last look at his enormous black boots and black leather trench-coat and then leave for the camping section a little further on. After a brief walk through the camping section I go to the kitchen appliance section. Both are equally useless and offer nothing that I could buy as a birthday present to myself. Inevitably, I find myself wandering aimlessly towards the frozen food aisle.

In the middle of the supermarket a woman in a Carrefour T-shirt is stood behind a promotional stall. As I pass she holds a tray of meat up to me and smiles.

'Can I interest you in a delicious piece of kangaroo steak?'

'Kangaroo?'

'It's really delicious. You should try some. We have a delicious recipe leaflet.'

'I'm not very good in the kitchen.'

'It's in four easy-to-follow steps. Take a look.'

She holds out a leaflet to me and I'm forced to stop my shopping trolley.

'Would you like to taste the kangaroo steak?'

'What does it taste like?'

'Have you ever had emu?'

'No. I've not.'

'It isn't so very different to the taste of emu. But it isn't so different to beef.'

She skewers a cube of meat with a wooden toothpick and holds it out to me.

'Kangaroo meat is one of the healthiest meats on earth.'

I take the toothpick and eat the meat. It tastes like beef, with maybe a little venison.

'Delicious stuffed with mushrooms and rosemary, and served with our delicious port sauce reduction.'

I nod my head and push my shopping trolley away in the direction of the frozen food aisle. For some reason the spaghetti Bolognese microwave meals have moved three freezers further along the aisle past the frozen mini-pizzas. At first I think it's just a mistake, but the chicken curry microwave meals have moved, too. Sometimes products are moved and I prefer the new location to the old location, but separating the microwave meals like that seems ridiculous. I shake my head and catch the eye of a man pushing a small shopping trolley like the one I've chosen – the shopping trolley that's clearly been designed specifically for single people. He looks confused and stands at the freezer where the spaghetti Bolognese microwave meals used to be.

'Are you looking for the spaghetti Bolognese microwave meals?' I ask.

He turns and pauses, as if to admit to such a thing would be to admit to a more general, unnameable defeat.

'Yes.'

'They've moved them. They're in that freezer there.' I point to the freezer further along the aisle.

'Oh. Right. Thank you.'

'The chicken curries are in that one.' I point again, at the freezer containing the chicken curries, and the man nods his head sheepishly, his eyes drawn down to the microwave meals stacked in my own shopping trolley. I think about saying something else, but instead I just wander away towards the alcohol section and consider the possibility of returning to the camping section and the electrical section. As I'm passing across the centre aisle I notice the goth tasting a piece of kangaroo meat at the promotional stall in the middle of the supermarket. He's nodding his head thoughtfully as he's chewing and the woman is discussing the recipe leaflet. Seeing the goth chewing a piece of kangaroo meat is possibly more disturbing than seeing him considering the purchase of a birthday card. I want to stop and watch him again, but my shopping trolley would be in the way of the other shoppers and sooner or later there would be a collision. Instead, I make my way to the alcohol section, slowing a little to look up at the signs above each of the aisles. The man I spoke to in the frozen food aisle is standing in front of the whisky shelves. I linger by the shelves of red wine and wait for him to leave. I can't help wondering if two men have ever become friends in a supermarket, but I know it would be ridiculous to start a conversation with a stranger for the second time in such a situation.

I pretend to choose a bottle of Cabernet Sauvignon and watch him leave. I'm probably never going to see him again, no matter how often I return to the supermarket. As he reaches the tills, I realise there are no other customers in the alcohol section. No one likes to linger in the alcohol section. I'm going to be allowed to choose something for my birthday at leisure.

After five minutes I decide on a bottle of the banana rum I used to drink on a holiday I took to Tenerife with Anthea. On my way out of the supermarket I stop at the pharmacy and pick up my prescription before taking a taxi back to the villa. I haven't really enjoyed looking for a birthday present for myself, but at least the taxi-driver has no inclination to speak. We sit in silence and I listen to the windscreen wipers and the rain, his eyes glancing in the rear-view mirror as I wash four painkillers down with a mouthful of banana rum. I think about telling him about the woman promoting kangaroo meat in the supermarket. Perhaps he'd like to hear about something like that.

37

I CAN'T REMEMBER much about my holiday in Tenerife with Anthea. I even confuse the hotel swimming pool with another swimming pool somewhere else, I don't know where, another holiday.

I finish the last of the banana rum and stare at the wall, at the reflection of the night sky in the television screen. I smoke a cigarette and then get up and go into the other room and sit in the wicker chair without bothering to turn on any of the lights. The moon is shining on the sea. After what seems like a long time I stand up and look across the dunes. The sand is the colour of grey dust and the marram grass is blowing in the wind.

I open the window and look along the beach where the woman sometimes stands at the edge of the sea. The cold air feels good on my skin and I can smell the slightly disgusting smell of the seaweed on the beach.

When I close the window I accidentally knock the bonsai tree off the windowsill with my elbow and the pot smashes loudly on the floor. I stand and stare at the broken shards of china scattered across a carpet of soil. I step away backwards and turn the light on. The bright white light hurts my eyes and I have to shade the glare with my hand, but I can see that the little tree has landed upside down and taken the full weight of the pot and the soil. The trunk has been broken in half. I scoop the clump of soil and roots in the palms of my hands and place the broken tree back on the windowsill.

The tree's two halves are being held together by a few thin sinews of splintered wood. I look down at the broken pieces of pot and move the wicker chair back away from the soil, glancing at my reflection in the window. My skin looks pale and dirty, as though it has been rubbed with newspaper. I didn't bother to have a wash before I went to the supermarket. The thought never occurred to me.

I get up and go into the bathroom to run a bath of cold water, undressing as I wait for the bath to fill. The water looks cold; heavy and solid and blue. I used to boil a kettle to wash in the sink, but the kettle has broken, too. I try not to think about it and lower my feet and legs into the water, then slide my whole body under the surface. The shock of the cold makes me gasp for breath. It's almost impossible to control my breathing. My chest heaves in spasms like a crying child's as I struggle to swallow a mouthful of air. Eventually I manage to breath more deeply and slowly and to calm my heart from pounding against my ribcage.

I realise that if you lie perfectly still it would be impossible to know whether you're lying in a bath of hot water or cold water. Your skin's unable to differentiate between the two. It's only when you move that the shock of the cold returns to wash against you.

I reach for the sliver of soap by the taps, slowly rising out of the water to stretch out my arm with the smallest of movements. The act of lathering my body is unpleasant, every sudden movement and splash catching my breath. I rush to scrub myself clean and sink back under the surface. Again, when my heart has calmed, it is impossible to tell whether the water is warm or cold. I rest my head against the porcelain and stare at the ceiling. There are as many knots of abandoned dusty cobwebs as there are in the other rooms. I purse my lips and blow at the ceiling and the cobwebs stir in the current of air, the slight effort of my stomach muscles causing a cold ripple of water to wash against my chest and neck. My heart beats a little faster, slows and calms, each systole creating a small undulation in the shallow water above my sternum.

I don't move until I start to shiver. My feet and hands are starting to ache and go numb. I stand up and wash my legs and genitals and between my buttocks and then rinse myself off. By the time I've finished drying myself and putting on my clothes, my skin has flushed with a radiant warmth. I put on my slippers and go into the bedroom containing my father's boxes, sit in the chair and light a cigarette. I'm not sure which of the boxes I've yet to look through. Perhaps I've looked through them all. I would have to search through them to see which of their lids are still taped together. From where I'm sitting, it's impossible to tell.

I finish my cigarette and think about throwing the burning stub into one of the opened boxes stacked against the wall. It would be nice to watch them burn, to watch their contents slowly disintegrate, consumed in flames. I let my arm fall from the chair and drop the cigarette on to the floorboards. My limbs and muscles are still glowing in a luxuriant warmth from the cold bath. I close my eyes and feel myself drifting to sleep. Joy is standing with the woman from the beach in a room overgrown with weeds. Both are indistinguishable in their beauty, their eyes shining blackly in the darkness. Joy looks at me, her face expressionless as I move towards her.

I wake up still sitting in the chair, my chin slumped on my chest. The light from the bare light-bulb is too bright and I can barely open my eyes. I don't know how long I've been asleep. The cigarette stub has burnt out on the floor. I go into the other bedroom and get into bed fully clothed, still wearing my slippers, the soles dirty with the soil from the broken bonsai tree pot.

I wake up in the early hours of the morning; again in the afternoon and late afternoon. I stare at the reflection of the sky in the television screen, bright white clouds moving from left to right. I can hear the gulls calling over the villa. The wind and the clouds and the occasional bluster of rain on the window is enough to pass the time. Once or twice a wood-louse has crawled from under the skirting board. I look at the hole where it appeared. I convince myself that I can see something moving, grey legs twitching in a constant rhythm, bodies huddled together. I get up off the mattress and pick up a discarded fork from the floor, then kneel and ram it again and again into the hole under the skirting board. I was right. The fork has skewered a woodlouse. I hold it upside down and watch its legs running in the air. Its punctured innards form a little brown bubble cupped by its shell. I put the fork on the floor and stand on the insect, then climb back into bed.

I look at the television screen, at the clouds moving from left to right. After a while I fall back to sleep.

38

I HAVE TO dig out the perimeter wall almost every day during the last weeks of autumn. It has rained for a month
and I'm forced to fight a losing battle with a seemingly end-
less invasion of insects. They crawl from every crack in the
walls and floorboards, and I have to check the hairs on my
arms and legs, rifle through my hair, watching for anything
falling on to the floor. Most of the insects are virtually invis-
ible, smaller than lice and as difficult to catch between your
fingers. I started to wonder whether they'd hatched from the
bonsai tree soil after the pot had broken on the floor. The walls
in the small bedroom are covered with little brown smears
where I've squashed them with my finger and spread their
legs and bodies across the paintwork. I don't have a television and so there isn't much to do but kill insects. Sometimes
I hold the flame from my cigarette lighter to them, but the
approaching light gives them the chance to scuttle away and
hide.

At least I can't hear them like the rats downstairs in the
kitchen. Besides, the infection in my jaw has spread into my
skull and I've started to go deaf, a painful deafness that sometimes pierces the centre of my head like a spike. I feel like I've
left it too late to go to the doctor. I wouldn't know what to say.
There's always the possibility that things might be worse than I
thought. Besides, I can convince myself that things are starting

to improve, even though I haven't been able to eat much and my weight loss has increased.

I raise my hands in front of my face and look at the dirt under my fingernails. My hands and wrists look thin and withered. I've been digging all afternoon in the rain. I take off my wet clothes and sit in the wicker chair in my pyjama trousers and a thick jacket. Some of the bonsai tree's soil has turned into mud and dirty water where it's fallen under the leaking ceiling.

I smoke a cigarette and look out of the window. Before it started to rain I saw the young woman walking along the beach followed by the boy darting around her like an excited dog. Again she stopped close to the reach of the waves and stared at the sea before retracing her footprints. I watched her while I was digging. On her way back she looked at me. I thought about following her, but the boy would have caught sight of me as we made our way through the dunes.

I stand up at the window and look for her footprints. If they hadn't been washed away in the rain I could have followed them to the other side of the woods beyond the road. I go into the bathroom and urinate. My urine splashing silently into the toilet bowl reminds me that I can't hear anything. I flush the toilet and watch the water foam and disappear without a sound. I can only hear the dull internal humming that accompanies me everywhere I go.

I take some tablets, a more or less random combination of everything I have available, and lie on the mattress. I turn the television on and watch a series of broken images from a daytime soap opera flicker across the screen, each freezing into fragmented distortions of colour: a woman's face in close-up; a discarded high-heel shoe; a sneering man sitting on a leather sofa. I don't move for hours except to light a cigarette. When it goes dark I turn on the light so that I can watch for insects crawling up my arms and legs.

It isn't long before I feel something struggling through the hairs below my calf – a small, black insect with a pointed, squirming carapace extending beyond its hind legs. I squash it with my finger and rub its body into a brown smear across my shin. I closely inspect both legs, running my fingers over the skin, then check the mattress and the sheets. I brush what looks like a dead mosquito on to the floor with some crumbs of dirt and lie back down. An empty chair flickers across the television screen; a woman's hand frozen in a blurred gesture.

I turn my laptop on and think about looking to see if any of my friends are in the chatroom on THAILOVELINKS.COM, but for some reason I decide to check my emails. There are 248 unopened messages in my inbox. I scroll through them and delete them one by one. When I've finished, a small smiley face appears on the screen to congratulate me on my perfectly clean email account.

I stare at the screen for a few minutes. The smiley face disappears, reappearing a moment later to smile and congratulate me again. I decide to go on to PARTNERS.BE. The chatroom is virtually empty except for single men, and there's only one couple with their webcam turned on. I click on their webcam. A man's hands are prising apart a woman's buttocks, stretching the skin taut around her anus and vagina. The man leans into view and pushes his tongue deep into the woman's anus again and again while his fingers slide in and out of her vagina in a sawing motion.

The couple seem to be in a conversation with someone in the chatroom. The man turns to the camera and says something, before adjusting the position of the webcam. I stare at the blurred image on the screen, at the woman's distended breasts as the man disappears and the woman turns to look at the computer screen, her hand moving between her legs, her finger sliding between her labia and into her vagina before slowly circling over and around her clitoris.

The webcam must be positioned on a tripod at the end of the bed. I look at the patterned wallpaper behind the headboard, at the clutter of objects on top of each of the small chest of drawers on either side of the bed. The woman lies back to stare into the camera, her mouth twisting into a grimace as her lips reveal her clenched teeth. The man reappears and kneels on the mattress, holding his flaccid penis towards his wife's face.

I click on the button to leave the chatroom and turn my computer off. I can feel an insect crawling up my leg. I inspect the hairs above my left ankle and check the mattress and the surrounding floorboards, but I can't find anything.

I lie back down on the mattress and look at the television screen. The image is badly distorted but I can see the right side of Marie-Pierre Mouligneau's face, her high cheekbone and short brown hair. The picture has frozen and she has been caught between expressions, her eyes half-closed and her mouth slightly open. She seems to be exhibiting a mood of cold indifference, or perhaps a barely suppressed wish to commit an act of violence.

I flick through the channels until I've reached the first of the adult channels. I can see what looks like blonde hair and the fabric of a bright pink bikini. At the bottom of the screen, blurred by a violet rectangle of pure colour, a large erect penis is entering a dark-skinned vagina. The flickering brown labia remind me of Joy's vagina and the greyish brown skin of her pubis and anus. The image starts to fade to a splice of grey and blue as Joy's face appears, her cheek bruised by the television's broken screen, her clear black eyes lowered to something unseen.

I stare at the screen, at Joy's dark eyes and painted red lips, as the shifting colours play across the walls and ceiling in a nauseous kaleidoscope. Her face turns upwards, her gaze lifting as she opens her mouth to expose her tongue and the back of her throat. Again, the image freezes in a blur, the delicate skin of Joy's neck stained with a darkening crimson.

I think about turning the television off, but instead I watch as Joy's breasts are bitten and slapped, as her vagina and anus are penetrated simultaneously in a flickering, broken narrative.

39

I HAVE TO admit certain things to myself. I'd hoped that the ghostwriter's book would make me famous, and now I'm hoping that my own book will make me famous, even though it has been rejected by the third publisher I've sent it to, this time a relatively small publishing house. A letter of regret was waiting for me at the post office. They have made suggestions by way of an apology, that the manuscript is too short, that the public expects a certain size and weight from a book, as you would with a bag of potatoes perhaps.

And so I will have to delay the dénouement. Not that there's going to be much of a dénouement. I already know that my book is a failure. I always knew that it was going to be a failure. I won't so much finish the book as abandon it half finished. It would seem silly to construct a clever little ending now.

I can't help but to wonder whether I'm sitting here waiting for the sea to destroy the villa. There's a high tide today and the sea is washing against the dunes. Perhaps that could be my book's dénouement. It almost seems too clever a construction. Occasionally a wave spills over the lip of sand at the edge of the beach. A shallow lake has formed beyond the perimeter wall.

I light a cigarette and open the window. The wind rushes into the room, damp and warm, stirring the dirt on the floor and blowing the ash from my cigarette. I watch the waves crashing silently at the foot of the biggest dune, a silence disturbed only by the unpleasant humming inside my head.

On my way home from the post office I stopped at the supermarket and bought all the products necessary to clean the villa: a mop and bucket, floor cleaning liquid, a sponge and scouring pads, garbage bags, a dust pan and brush, a robust wooden broom. For a while the purchases filled me with optimism, but I've done nothing except to look at them for three days now. I've decided that I'm going to make a start by sweeping the stairs. I used to like vacuum cleaning, the sense of accomplishment, but I no longer own a vacuum cleaner. I looked at some of the latest models in the supermarket and considered purchasing a somewhat beautiful new Dyson, but in the end I didn't bother.

Again, I decide to make a start. I look at the detritus strewn across the varnished wooden stairs. Dust, sand, knotted clumps of hair and unidentifiable pieces of plastic or paper. Only the wrapper from a slice of processed cheese is discernible. I finish my cigarette and start to sweep up with the little dustpan and brush that I've bought, one careful step at a time until I'm at the bottom of the stairs. Within five minutes I've finished and the stairs are perfectly clean. It's pleasing to have achieved so much in such a short space of time. The varnished wood is almost gleaming in the light. It's going to be a pleasure to walk up and down on them.

I look at the contents of the dustpan with a sense of triumph. A small insect the colour of a blood blister is crawling slowly through the dust. I watch it and realise there are two more, each one struggling through miniature mounds of dust and rubbish. I raise the dustpan to my face and peer over the rim. I think about killing them, but in the end I decide to empty the insects along with the rest of the contents of the dustpan into one of the black bin bags I've bought.

When I carry the bin bag out into the garden, the young boy is standing on a dune by the perimeter wall. He has a strangely disgusting expression on his face and makes a gesture in the air as he says something. I don't know what to say. I shake my head as I place the bin bag against the wall in a corner of the garden and tell him that I can't hear anything. Perhaps I could strangle him. Disposing with a body would be a relatively easy affair. I could cut his body into pieces in the bath. I would finally have a reason to purchase one of the expensive Japanese sushi knives I've always wanted. I can imagine leaving an arm in a field in Florennes, half of a leg on the outskirts of Verviers. That sort of thing must happen all the time, at least if the programmes on television are to be believed. I don't know. I find it difficult enough to kill an insect.

As I'm about to go back inside, I see the young boy's lips moving. I presume that he's asking me about the black bin bag. I tell him that I'm sorting through the rubbish, that the villa was my father's and that I'm planning to decorate the interior. I can feel him watching me as I walk back across the garden towards the villa. I think about looking at him as I slide the patio doors shut, perhaps to show him that I find his presence vaguely annoying. But instead I wander out of the living room, shuffling in my slippers across the dirty floor.

Even the clean wooden stairs aren't enough to console me. I pause in the hall to look at them. I don't know why I bothered to clean them. They boy's presence has ruined everything. I raise my leg on to the first step and lean against the banister. With an effort I start to climb the stairs, one step at a time, right foot first, slowly transferring my weight from leg to leg. As I reach the top, a muffled thud and a series of dull crashing sounds penetrate my deafness. I walk towards the small bedroom. Shards of broken glass are scattered across the floor. A large stone lies against the skirting board. The window has been smashed. I lean around the door to look. The dunes look suddenly clean and fresh in the empty rectangle of space.

I shield myself behind the door and stare at the floor, my eyes automatically searching for insects in the rubbish. The dust is as thick as wool and I can see something moving not far from a piece of broken glass. I raise my foot and squash it against the floorboards. Its innards are barely sufficient to moisten the sole of my slipper.

40

I DREAM THAT the boy is Joy's son and that I'm still accused of his mother's murder. I take him to the circus in an attempt to assuage his hatred of me. An abstract notion of the word 'Bruges' hovers over a confusion of buildings that are both familiar and unpleasantly strange. I recognise the cathedral tower and the feel of the cold wind blowing across the stone square from the river; but between the buildings that seem in some way familiar, I'm able to discern the beach and the dunes, the flat grey sea and the wash of the gently rising waves. We take our seats in a confused auditorium constructed on the rippled sand of a beach, and realise that something terrible has already happened, the audience is craning their necks to see down into the pit, some people are starting to stand up and shout. A large baboon has died during an aerial acrobatics performance. Its body lies limp on a small wooden stage in the middle of the circus tent and a doctor in a surgical mask is inserting a medical instrument into the animal's chest. When the doctor shakes his head and covers the baboon's dead body with a sheet, the crowd starts to hiss and boo wildly. I realise that I've forgotten to shield the boy's eyes or to distract him from the horribly sad scene below. As I turn to him the lights go out. The women and girls in the audience start to scream histrionically. I try to laugh to comfort the boy but I can't see his face and I don't know if he can see my face. I feel for him in the blackness but I can only feel an empty chair and the other people sitting around us, their unmoving heads and shoulders. I stand up and start to push my way through the crowd. Everybody is suddenly rushing in the opposite direction and I have to fight and wrestle through the crush of bodies. I trip and fall on to the wet sand and it takes all of my strength not to be pushed down beneath blow after blow of flailing arms and charging knees. But I'm overwhelmed and I sink down under the flow of bodies pushing for an unseen exit. As I'm trampled to the edge of consciousness, I see the boy's body lying at the side of me, as still as the dead baboon's. I reach for him and he turns his head. I'm about to say something as an elephant tramples through the crowd, its deafening trumpet silencing the screams, its enormous feet crushing my pelvis as it stamps maliciously through the tangle of human limbs. I groan in agony and try to crawl away to safety but I'm unable to move my legs. Blood seeps from my shattered pelvis, covering my hands as I struggle like a beached swimmer in a dark viscous pool rising across the sand towards the boy. I look at the bright red smears on my palms and fingers, at the blood dripping down my wrists, the only colour visible in the darkness of the circus tent. We need to escape, I say. I'm bleeding. The lion's coming. The boy's face is placid, indifferent, and at that moment I want to kill him, but I know that he is going to succeed in killing me first. I roll on to my stomach and try to push myself away from him. My trousers are heavy with blood, and I can feel it soaking through to my genitals as I pull myself under the tangle of limbs and bodies to shelter in a half destroyed and partially buried wooden cabinet in a corner of the circus tent. My penis and scrotum are sticky with congealing blood. I unfasten my trousers and pinch with my fingernails at a disgusting clot forming in the eye of my glans like an obscene ruby.

The woman I've seen on the beach crawls into the cabinet I'm hiding in, grabbing frantically at a dozen lace skirts that she's wearing, raising them to reveal the dark, purplish skin of her pudenda, spreading her legs and parting her labia for me to enter her. Do you know where the boy is? she asks as she reaches to steer my bloody penis into her vagina. You should kill him before he kills you. I look down at my penis as it disappears into the convoluted mouth of the woman's swollen vulva, more like a baboon's than a woman's. I can sense the lion approaching in the darkness and I realise there are no doors attached to the cabinet we're hiding inside. The circus tent is silent and empty and I can somehow see the waves washing between the familiar buildings and along the streets in the distance. The audience has managed to escape. A few crushed bodies lie scattered across the beach like indistinguishable piles of clothing. The woman pulls me into her, writhing her hips against my shattered pelvis and ignoring my grimaces. I grab her throat to try to stop her but my hands are too weak and I can barely manage to clench my fingers around her oesophagus. She laughs and moans with pleasure as a strong hand grabs my shoulder and I turn around to see the baboon crouching behind me, his long pink phallus sticking in the air like a horsewhip. I want both of you to fuck me, the woman says, rubbing her fingers over her clitoris as the baboon shoulders himself behind me and slides his thin penis into her vagina. I can feel his coarse fur scratching my back, his bulbous, muscular stomach slapping against my buttocks as our cocks rub together. I try again to strangle the woman and wrap my numbed hands around her throat, my arms as weak as a child's. As I'm about to ejaculate, the lion appears, closer, not far from the cabinet, its enormous head moving slowly, almost imperceptibly, in a terrifying nod. The baboon jerks his snout under my armpit, his lips fluttering from his teeth as he tastes the air. I push my penis deep inside the woman, feeling the muscles of her vagina relax and clasp as the lion charges forwards towards us.

41

O N CHRISTMAS DAY I'm barely capable of getting out
of bed. I boil a cup of water in the microwave to make
coffee and sit in the wicker chair. A light, wintry rain blows
through the empty window frame, small greying flakes of ice
wetting the windowsill as they melt, broken snowflakes catching on the withered branches of the dead bonsai tree. I watch
as a pool of water forms across the windowsill, threatening
to spill over the edge and drip on to the floor. I put on my
coat and the Russian hat I found in one of my father's boxes,
measuring the hours with cigarettes. By the late afternoon I
find it almost impossible to resist the urge to celebrate. I fill a
glass with whisky and walk around the villa quietly humming
and singing to myself to warm myself up. I imagine a knock
at the door, the young woman from the beach wrapped in her
headscarf, her dark eyes and soft skin framed in an oval of
cloth and black hair.

I was wondering if you'd like to go to the circus this
evening? she says. I have two tickets and I thought you might
like to come with me. I would love to go to the circus with you,
I say, as we leave for the train hand in hand. Bruges is such a
beautiful city. Look at the cathedral, she says, it's really ro-
mantic, isn't it? Let's walk around the empty streets together;
everyone's at home and it looks really beautiful and quiet in
the snow and the yellow streetlights.

I sit back in the wicker chair. The dunes are beginning to drain of colour. I drink a second glass of whisky and sing a Christmas carol, my voice quiet, breaking on the high notes and drowned by my deafness.

> *Douce nuit, sainte nuit*
> *Dans les cieux, l'astre luit*
> *Le mystère annoncé s'accomplit*
> *Cet enfant sur la paille endormi*
> *C'est l'amour infini!*
> *C'est l'amour infini!*

When I've finished I stare out of the window at the dunes and the beach and the darkening expanse of the sea stretching to meet the early evening sky. You are beautiful, I say. We are sitting on a bench in an empty square and the woman from the beach has removed her scarf to reveal her hair. She smiles and looks away at the snow and the soft lights flickering in the windows of the old stone buildings.

She leans towards me, her fingers gently stroking my face. We embrace on the bench in the snow, holding one another in the silence of the empty square. I sing the Christmas carol again, my cheek resting against her hair, breathing the smell of her hair as I sing.

I imagine her face as I stare out of the window at the wintry dunes undulating in the drifting sleet down to the beach. Sometimes it's necessary to invent a little company once in a while. Perhaps she would be kind enough to accompany me more often as I wander around the villa.

I search my jacket pockets for a packet of cigarettes and go into the small bedroom. In the last of my father's boxes I found a large, relatively old mobile phone. The letters on the keypad have almost worn away and the screen has been slightly damaged. I turn it over in the palm of my hand and look at the dust that has collected between the plastic seams and around the translucent rubber keys. My father's skin cells; his dried mucous and spermatozoa.

I turn the mobile phone on. The screen illuminates and the word 'Bonjour' appears. I press the menu button, and then the messages button, but there are no messages in the outbox, and only one in the inbox – from his mobile phone company wishing him a happy new year. In the phonebook there are only the numbers for his doctor, lawyer and three other people. None of the names mean anything to me. Three months before his death he called a number that is only recorded in the call log. The conversation lasted for seven minutes and twenty-two seconds.

The battery goes dead as I'm contemplating calling the number. I put the phone back in the box where I found it. I don't know how it came to be packed away, buried beneath so much junk at the very back of the room. Perhaps my father used to sift through his possessions, too, rearranging the boxes as he went along just as I have been doing. I light another ciga-rette and take a handful of tablets, imagining them travelling down my throat to my stomach. I can almost feel them enter-ing my bloodstream, like warm, melting lozenges.

I look up at the broken window and rest the back of my head against the cold interior wall, rolling the uneven crown of my skull against the hard plaster. I can see the sky, an oblong of grey cloud shifting indeterminately over a flat, whitish yellow. The changing reflections of yellow and orange on the under-sides of the blurry white clouds tell me that the sun is low in the sky. The words 'bruised egg' come to mind. Perhaps that's how best to describe the sky at this moment.

42

O N THE FIRST of January I receive a text message from my mobile phone company wishing me a happy new year. It arrives at 12:57 in the afternoon.

I'm sitting looking at the dunes. I've replaced the broken window with strips of adhesive tape stretched from one side of the frame to the other. The dunes and the beach look blurred and fragmented through the strips of twisted cellulose. The wind is blowing through the gaps in the tape, and the sudden changes in the air pressure repeatedly threaten to destroy the entire construction.

Last night I dreamt that Joy shot me in the forehead with a gun I'd found inside one of my father's boxes. She was standing with her back to the wall and I slipped my finger around the trigger and waved the revolver in the air. She looked worried and flinched as I pointed the gun at her face and pretended to press the trigger, making the sound of a gunshot with my mouth and laughing. To appease her complaints I asked her if she'd like to play Russian roulette and spun the cylinder before holding the barrel to my temple. I hadn't thought to look how many bullets were in the gun, whether any of the chambers were empty. A loud metallic click pierced my ear as I pressed the trigger. I smiled and held the gun out to Joy. She took it reluctantly and held it like a dying bird cradled in the palms of her hands. I watched as she wrapped her fingers around

the wooden grip, sliding her index finger slowly and carefully through the trigger guard before calmly raising the gun to
point the barrel at my head. As I'm about to say something I
see her hand move and hear a terrifying scream that forces me
to turn my head and close my eyes. I almost think that she was
only pretending to press the trigger, but I'm lying on the floor
and I can feel the warm blood pouring out of the back of my
head.

I light a cigarette and look across the beach to someone walking in the distance by the edge of the sea. After what seems like
a long time, the greying figure fades to nothing. Hours pass.
Occasionally I ask myself a question, or say something that I
might find interesting. Two crows fly over the coast, swoop-
ing on the dunes before disappearing from sight. I tell myself
that they are intelligent creatures; that they've been observed
using various tools to find grubs and to break the shells of
molluscs.

Late in the afternoon, I go into the other bedroom and pour
a can of soup into a glass to heat it in the microwave. I was
pleased with myself when I stumbled on the glass idea. A glass
is easier to wash under the tap and you don't need to use a
spoon. After I've finished my soup, I take off my slippers and
put on my shoes and go out into the garden with my spade.

The perimeter wall has been virtually destroyed. I look at
the concrete blocks scattered across the ground, at the sand
under my feet where there were flower beds and a patio. The
air feels damp and heavy, warm for early January. A light rain
starts to fall as I'm digging, but light enough to feel pleasant.
After an hour I hear something and look up instinctively – a
muffled sound that penetrates my deafness. A stone has hit the
perimeter wall and landed in the sand six feet away from me.
I look at it, momentarily confused, bent over with my spade

buried in the mound of sand I'm trying to move. A pebble from the beach, half the size of a fist. I think about looking to see who has thrown it. I wait for a moment, turn my head a little towards the beach. I can feel my heart beating in my chest and I'm scared of a stone hitting me in the face, even though I know it's being thrown by a boy.

I continue digging, hesitantly sliding the blade into the wet sand. I pretend not to be concerned, and glance over my shoulder across the dunes. I can't see anyone. As I look up I'm hit in the face and my head is knocked backwards. Everything goes black and I fall on my hands and knees, my head screaming with a pain I can hear like white noise behind my eyes. I don't move; I stay like that, on my hands and knees, with my head resting against the sand.

When the pain starts to subside a little, I take a deep breath to calm myself down. I can't see. I'm unable to open my eyes. The pain gets worse when I try. My left eye is streaming with blood. I can feel it dripping from my cheek. Without thinking, I cover my head with my arm, in case another stone hits me, and crawl behind the nearest dune. I realise that I don't know where I am and wonder why I'm surrounded by sand. Am I lost in a desert? I shake my head and struggle to understand what I'm doing here. I don't move for what seems a long time. The wind is blowing against my face and body, ruffling the collar of my coat.

Why is everything so quiet? After a while I can feel the wound on my cheek starting to harden as the blood dries into a scab. I curl up into the foetal position, resting my head against the relatively warm dune, and decide to stay where I am until I'm able to understand things a little more clearly. I'm nauseous and I feel as though I could easily fall to sleep. A bird sings from somewhere in the sky, a beautifully melancholic song that I'm able to understand. I realise that I've been dreaming. I must have fallen asleep. I settle my head into the dune again, oblivious to everything.

When I wake again, my confusion slowly dissolves. I know who I am, where I am, but it takes a few moments to realise why I am lying outside in the sand. I don't know how long I have slept for. It is the middle of the day. The sun is shining and I can hear the birds in the sky.

I open my eyes enough to see the concrete wall not far from my feet. Straining to see causes a tremendous pain in my skull and left eye to flare up again, like a hot needle inserted into the pupil, and I have to close my eyes until it goes away. I wait, feeling for my spade in the sand. I can't find it. I thought it was lying next to me but the wind might have buried it. When I open my eyes again, a woman is standing by my feet looking down at me. She's wearing a floral dress and black wellington boots. I look at her pale white legs, almost greyish-blue, dotted with purplish pink spots where she has shaved the hairs just below her knees. Her summer dress confuses me a little and I immediately feel hot and uncomfortable lying in the sun.

The woman's mouth is moving as though she's saying something. I look at her hair hanging down from all around her face because she's leaning over me. It takes a few seconds for me to remember that I've lost my hearing.

'I'm deaf,' I say, before correcting myself: 'I can't hear anything.'

The woman says something else and kneels down beside me, her eyes fixed on the wound at the side of my head.

'Someone threw a stone at me,' I say in an attempt to guess what she might be asking. 'But I think I'm all right.'

She purses her lips and narrows her eyes in sympathy, saying something else, perhaps another question, as her arm gestures towards the villa. I shake my head and tell her that I can't hear what she's saying. The woman smiles warmly and grabs me under my arm to help me to my feet. When I stand up I can see the spade. I try to bend down to pick it up but the young woman tightens her grip on my arm. Perhaps she thinks I was losing my balance.

'I don't want to lose my spade,' I say.

The woman bends down and picks the spade up for me. She's saying something, her face is tilted to mine and her lips are moving. I don't understand why she insists on speaking when I've told her that I can't hear a thing that she's saying.

'I can't hear what you're saying,' I say. 'I can't hear anything – I'm deaf.'

The woman smiles and points at something behind me. I turn around to look. A black dog with a stick in its mouth is standing wagging its tail at her. I realise that the woman has been talking to her dog, perhaps instructing it to keep away from me.

She wraps my arm around her shoulders and holds me around the waist as we make our way towards the gate at the back of the villa. I already know why she's come to help me. Her son threw the stone, and confessed to her about what had happened later in the evening. Maybe he'd been worried that he'd killed me.

When we're in the villa I thank the woman for helping me. She looks around at the discarded rubbish strewn across the living room floor, at the stained bare walls and the single arm-chair facing an empty corner of the room.

'I'm sorry about the mess,' I say. 'I live upstairs. But I suppose I should tidy up a little.'

The woman winces and turns her head to a black bin bag full of rotting garbage. I think about apologising again and explaining that the authorities refuse to collect my household rubbish, but instead I close my eyes and gently palpate my skull. After a few seconds I feel the woman's hand stroking my shoulder.

'I'm sorry about the mess,' I say. 'You must think it's really disgusting.'

I open my eyes and look at her lips as she's saying something. In the middle of a sentence I see her lips and tongue form the word 'hospital'. I shake my head and say that I'm fine. The woman looks confused and makes a sign with her hands to indicate that she wants to write something on a piece of paper. I look around at the floor, at the discarded bottles of wine and whisky and vodka, at the crushed cans of beer, the ready-meal cartons – everything half buried in sand and dried mud. Nothing has changed since the detectives came to arrest me.

'I don't have anything to write with,' I say. 'I mean, I don't think that I have anything to write with.'

I look around again at the floor and the woman smiles weakly, feeling her dress to indicate that she has no pockets.

'Would you like me to come back later?' she asks.

I shake my head. 'I'm fine. Really.'

'You don't look fine.'

'It's nothing. I just have a headache.'

As we walk back towards the door where the dog is waiting, I tell her that I'm grateful that she came to help me, even though the truth is that I'm not. Thanking her is the least I can do. I'm surprised that anyone came to help me. But still, I find the woman's presence in the villa has an extremely unpleasant effect on me. I stand at the patio doors and watch as she walks across the garden and disappears with her dog beyond the dunes. When she's left I lock the door and vomit uncontrollably on to the living room floor. Retching until my stomach is completely empty, I wipe my mouth and lean against the wall to stop myself from falling, glancing at the regurgitated pieces of food I don't remember eating, before making my way slowly upstairs to bed.

43

THERE IS A knock at the door. I don't answer. I never answer the door. Usually it is a representative from an electricity company. They would be going from door to door, making sure to call at every house in the area. Whoever it is knocks for what seems like a long time. I lie in bed and wait for them to go away. They have no right to knock on the door like that. It was the same thing yesterday, and the day before that. At first I thought that it might have been the detectives that came to arrest me about Joy's murder. But they would have had someone with them to break open the door. A door is not a problem as far as the police are concerned.

I think about getting out of bed and looking out of the window to see if I can see someone standing below, but I don't want to move in case they hear me. When they knock again for what seems like a minute, I think about going downstairs and opening the door, going along with everything they say, nodding my head and agreeing with them, and at the last minute, when I'm just about to sign whatever piece of paper they've pushed in front of me, I'll say that I've changed my mind and shut the door in their face.

I close my eyes and try to calm myself down a little. I feel as if my head were submerged in a bath of water, each knock penetrating my deafness like a dull, metallic echo. My heart is beating heavily in my chest. For a moment I think that I can hear someone shouting my name. But I don't know if I'm just imagining these things. Either way, when I hear a voice, my first thought is of Joy. I picture her standing outside at the door, and then curse myself for being so ridiculous. Almost uncontrollably, I imagine her buried deep in the soil of the small church yard in Leuven, her skeleton as you would see it in a cross-section photograph of her grave: the white bones of her skull, ribcage, hands, legs and feet encased in the collapsed rectangle of her wooden coffin; the shallow layers of earth topped by ankle-length grass, their yellowish roots reaching down to filter the soil like the roots of water lilies seen from below.

As usual, I start to think about her putrefaction. I open my eyes and look at the ceiling. The paint has become yellowed with cigarette smoke. Brown stains show where the roof is leaking rain. The matted remains of a cobweb flutter on a draught of air in the corner. I listen to the almost absolute silence, the distant, unpleasant humming inside my head waiting for something to happen. My father's bedside clock on the windowsill says that it is ten fifty-seven. I look at the motionless second hand. The manufacturer's name is written on the face of the clock, but I've never bothered to read it and I'm too far away to read it now.

After what seems like a long time, I realise that whoever was knocking at the door has once again finally decided to give up and leave me alone. I think about getting out of bed to see if I can see them walking back to their car. I reach for my tablets and cigarettes, holding them in my hand for a moment and listening. The humming in my head could be described as the sound of a blast furnace heard from a certain distance. Occasionally, it will be disturbed by what I could describe as an audible shadow. After a while, it's easy to mistake these vague differences for silence.

I get up off the mattress and stand at the window, hiding

my body behind the wall so that I won't be seen, craning my neck and pressing my face close to the glass. I am a hunted animal, an old dying rabbit that cannot leave his burrow for fear of being eaten by a thousand wolves. Occasionally he will step outside to stretch his tired legs and sniff the air, to nibble at a piece of grass – but the slightest shift in the breeze will chase him back down his hole, where he sits in the dark and the damp, resting, wasting away, thinking of his life.

I light a cigarette and take a handful of tablets, lost in the memory of a cartoon I loved as a child: a happy community of rabbits, destroyed when their field is sold by the local farmer to a group of uncaring housing developers. What for hundreds of generations of rabbits had been a small patch of peace and tranquillity, a rolling field of long grass surrounded by woodland, is suddenly dug to mud by enormous yellow machines, and planted with row upon row of bricks and concrete – all in the name of what the most frightening animal of all calls progress.

And to think that I had played my part in the maintenance of this illusion of progress! I turn away from the window, disgusted with myself, and walk into the back bedroom, sitting in the wicker chair and looking at the dunes. I can already feel the first effects of the tablets I've taken as they dissolve in my stomach, the peripheries of my legs and arms melting like butter over a gentle heat. It rarely happens quite like this any more, and I want to savour the deliciousness of the moment. But after less than twenty seconds, whoever it is has started to knock at the door again.

I stand up and throw my cigarette on to the floor, knocking the wicker chair over as I storm out and across the hall into the room containing my father's boxes to look for the revolver I'd found, tearing open the boxes and emptying their contents on to the floor in a rage. Only when a little pile of belongings has grown around my feet, do I remember that the gun had appeared in a dream, and that I hadn't actually found one amongst my father's things. I lower my head to my chest and wait, and at the next bout of knocking slowly make my way down the stairs, defeated.

A woman in a black mackintosh, a professional woman of some kind, is standing outside. I don't say anything. I find myself wincing as she starts to say something, as though her words are causing me pain. She looks a little confused and I wonder whether she's a detective, whether she's come to take me to the police station again. Perhaps it would be reasonable for a female police officer to attend arrests with a male colleague but she insists on rejecting this inherent sexism by refusing to accept the help of a man and by going on her own to apprehend all suspects, whether male or female.

I shrug my shoulders a little. 'I can't hear a thing that you're saying,' I say. 'I'm deaf.'

The woman says something else and I shrug my shoulders again and shake my head. She takes a notepad and pen out of her bag and begins to write something down, holding it up to me when she's finished.

CAN I COME IN
FOR A CHAT?

Her writing is big and looks a little aggressive, the words written in capital letters and almost carved into the paper. I think about saying that I can't read, but I still don't know whether she's a detective and I don't want to annoy her.

'The living room's a little disgusting,' I say. 'I live upstairs and there's nowhere for us to sit. I don't have many guests coming to visit me.'

I look down at her feet. She's wearing sensible shoes. The

kind that a detective might wear. Black shoes, black stockings, black skirt, black mackintosh. Her stockings have been dusted with sand up to her ankles, so she probably has sand in her shoes, too, which means she'll be even more annoyed than she would be normally. I watch as she starts to write something down again. She crosses a word out and thinks for a moment, before tearing the page from the notepad and starting again on a clean sheet.

I'M FROM THE ADULT SERVICES
DEPARTMENT. I JUST CAME TO
SEE IF EVERYTHING WAS OK, IF
YOU NEED ANY HELP WITH
ANYTHING . . .

'I don't need anything,' I say. She starts to write again.

COULD WE GO SOMEWHERE
FOR A CHAT ABOUT THINGS?
I DON'T REALLY WANT TO
STAND ON YOUR DOORSTEP

'I don't understand what you want to talk to me about.'

YOU DON'T LOOK VERY
WELL RAYMOND

'I have a cold. I've had it for a few days now. I don't see why that should be of any concern to you.'

I THINK YOU NEED TO
SEE A DOCTOR

'I see the doctor nearly every week. I have a prescription.'

YOUR DOCTOR SAYS YOU'RE
REFUSING TREATMENT

'No. It's not true. For what?'

WE NEED TO TALK ABOUT
THESE THINGS, RAYMOND.
SHOULD WE GO AND SIT
IN MY CAR? WE COULD
GO FOR A COFFEE?

I don't know what to say. I lower my head and look at the woman's shoes again. They're slip-ons, with thick, rubber soles. I don't know if there was a particular reason for her choosing such an ugly pair of shoes, or whether her decision was based on more general considerations of practicality.

We find a café further along the coast on the outskirts of a small seaside resort I've never visited before. On the way she shows me her local authority identity card as a means of introducing herself, and I learn that her name is Gwendolyn.

As we arrive the sun is beginning to break through the clouds and so we sit at an outside table by the edge of the promenade. The rest of the tables are unoccupied. The street is empty, too; each of an assortment of small tourist shops is closed and shuttered, with not a single person in sight.

Gwendolyn takes out her pad and begins to write.

YOU NEED TO KNOW
THAT I'M HERE TO
HELP YOU RAYMOND

I think about it for a moment and light a cigarette. 'You sound like the woman I met on the television programme.'

WHAT TELEVISION
PROGRAMME?

'I was on a television programme. My wife was murdered and they wanted to interview me about it.'

Gwendolyn looks a little concerned by what I've said. Perhaps she's used to dealing with dangerous fantasists. I look at her, and follow her stare to a piece of litter blowing along the empty street: a crushed polystyrene takeaway carton sliding sideways along the opposite pavement and coming to rest against the remains of an abandoned flowerbed. As the waitress brings our cups of coffee, Gwendolyn starts to write another question in her notepad. I'm already getting tired of answering her questions. This particular method of communication is becoming increasingly irritating. She leans forward to show me what she's written.

YOU'VE BEEN
ON TELEVISION?

'Yes. My wife was a famous porn star. Her name was Joy Valentine, but of course I don't know if you would have heard of her or not. I suppose it depends on your tastes in pornography.'

I take a drink of coffee and finish my cigarette. It's almost impossible to interpret whether Gwendolyn watches pornography or not, but she shakes her head a little to suggest that she doesn't, and that she isn't familiar with the name Joy Valentine.

'She was from Thailand,' I say. 'We were married when I

was on holiday there, and she came to live in Belgium. My father's body was found in the villa the day before our wedding.'

Gwendolyn nods her head and gestures for me to continue with what I was saying, but there's nothing left for me to say. I think about the senseless course of what are sometimes called 'events', but I don't have anything more to say on the subject.

'In the end she was murdered by one of her fans,' I say. 'If you want to know anything else, you can read about it. Someone wrote a book. Of course, there's always the internet, too.'

Gwendolyn's vague look of disbelief makes me wonder whether any of what I've said actually happened. I have so few memories of Joy that it seems more than reasonable to suggest that I have fabricated the entire episode.

I stare at the table as a sudden amnesia threatens to overwhelm me. For some reason the little white coffee cup sitting on its little white saucer brings a certain amount of relief.

'I don't feel so good,' I say.

Gwendolyn purses her lips and smiles as she reaches across the table to hold my shaking hand. I nod my head mechanically and begin to cry. Gwendolyn reaches into her bag for a tissue and flicks through her notepad to point at what she's already written.

YOU NEED TO KNOW
THAT I'M HERE TO
HELP YOU RAYMOND

I count three tears, only one of which manages to gain enough momentum to drip from my face. I've never found it very easy to cry. Perhaps the tear ducts are as susceptible to damage as the vas deferens. I wipe my eyes and thank Gwendolyn for her kind words. The world seems a little clearer to me now. I know that I will gladly accept whatever help is offered to me. For the moment I am able to think with a relative degree of clarity.

'I'm scared that I have cancer,' I say. 'The doctor suggested that I see a specialist at the hospital . . .'

Gwendolyn starts to write something in her notepad.

IT'S PROBABLY NOTHING.
DON'T WORRY

I nod my head in agreement and look around, amazed at the new found sense of the world the very briefest of cries has given me. The flickering light falling on the polished metal table seems imbued with a special significance I'm only now able to grasp. I run my fingers over the spiralling metal patterns glimmering warmly in the afternoon sunlight. I know that I'm going to be admitted to a psychiatric clinic, and that I will quietly acquiesce to its proposal, thereby negating the necessitation for legal formality. Perhaps I will never see the villa again. I only wish that things could have been different.

PART FOUR

44

THE ROOM I have been given is small. The walls are painted a peach colour and the carpet is blue. There is a bedside cabinet on one side of the bed, and a wardrobe on the other. Beside the wardrobe there is a framed reprint of a Monet water lily painting hanging on the wall.

I lie in bed and look at the small rectangular window. Sometimes the sun shines on the glass in the late afternoon and the patina of dirt sparkles like flakes of gold. The glass is thick and of the kind inlaid with squares of metal wire so that it doesn't break into shards very easily. I've been allowed to walk almost all the way around the building, but I wasn't able to find my small window amongst all the others. There were no distinguishing features.

During the day I'm taken to another room – a communal sitting room. There are eight chairs along one wall and eight chairs along the opposite wall. The chairs don't have arms and the sponge seats and backs are covered with a rose-coloured fabric that's becoming worn and faded. I sit in a chair against the wall facing the door, five chairs from the window and below a piece of paper stuck to the notice board reminding everyone to take their cups back to the kitchen when they've finished with them. The building reminds me of an old people's home, except that the smell of overcooked vegetables has been replaced with the smell of unnameable chemicals more reminiscent of a hospital.

From my chair I can see almost the whole of a tree outside in the small garden. I watch the branches swaying in the wind and the bark darkening to black in the rain. I've never realised how long it takes for a tree to grow back its leaves after winter. Clusters of purplish green buds appear, then nothing for months. Occasionally, a gardener comes to sweep the leaves and dead branches from the grass. Sometimes I can hear him when I'm in my room, his rake dragged across the ground on the other side of the wall.

I don't understand why there is usually only me sitting in the sitting room, or why I'm the only one who seems to be taken there after I've eaten the disgusting breakfast they force me to eat. Perhaps it's because I have no visitors. The nurses seem to look at me a certain way, their eyes a little misty, a familiar smile crossing their lips as they help me out of bed and into my wheelchair. By now they know to deposit me in the chair against the wall facing the door, five chairs from the window and below the piece of paper stuck to the notice board, where I can sit and look at the tree. Occasionally I write. The doctor has said that he will provide me with all the writing materials I require. He says there is an old typewriter that I can use in my room, so that I don't disturb anyone, or else I can write on paper with a pen in the sitting room. On Fridays the doctor usually asks if he can read a page or two of something I've written. He's given me a book about the second world war. He says that I should learn a little history. The second world war is his particular fascination.

On the whole I like living in the hospital. There are people to talk to during the evening meal, and the rest of the time you can occupy yourself more or less as you wish. At dinner, I sit at a table in the corner with a man called Eric. He's young and looks like an actor preparing for the role of Jesus. He has pale white skin that looks as though it's been polished with newspaper, and maintains the kind of facial hair that is somewhere between stubble and a short beard. We've agreed to be friends with one another when we get out of the hospital. He used to live in Leuven. I asked him which supermarket he went to and he said that he used to go to Match on Bondgenotenlaan street. I asked him if he'd ever seen the woman with the short brown hair tied in a ponytail. She usually worked on one of the checkouts and she was very pretty. We once had a conversation about a particular brand of washing-up liquid I was buying, and after that we always made sure to say hello to one another. I asked Eric if he ever went to the Carrefour Hypermarché but he said that he didn't like Carrefour. I told him that I like Carrefour Hypermarché, but that I like going to Match sometimes because they have really interesting special offers. Eric shook his head and said that it's good that we can disagree about things and still remain friends. I said that I knew what he meant, that going to a new supermarket can be a really strange experience. The first time I went to a Delhaize supermarket I left without buying anything. The aisles were too confusing for someone who had never been to a Delhaize supermarket before. Eric agreed with me and said that he'd never been to a Delhaize supermarket either.

Sometimes Eric doesn't come to the dining room and I have to eat on my own. I've thought about saying something to the man who sits alone at a table near to the fire exit. He always leaves halfway through his meal to go and smoke a cigarette in his room. I know that he goes to his room to smoke his cigarette because I can hear each of the corridor doors opening and closing all the way along the corridor, then around the corner and along the next corridor. The sound of the corridor doors opening and closing is particularly irritating. You can hear them all through the night and the sound wakes you up at least once or twice an hour. All of the patients in the hospital seem to need to go to the toilet with a ridiculous frequency. You can hear the toilets flushing, too, and the water tumbling down the pipes like a raging torrent passing through the walls. It's impossible to sleep. I don't know how anyone sleeps.

I've thought about asking Eric why he doesn't sometimes come to eat in the dining room. I always go to eat in the dining room. Everyone is a little subdued and it makes for a pleasant atmosphere. Besides, I like the soup. The soup is always very good.

45

I'VE BEEN SITTING alone in my favourite chair all afternoon. The gardener hasn't been to rake up the leaves and
the dead branches. Perhaps it's no longer necessary. I don't
know. I can't see the grass from where I'm sitting.

It's raining again. I look at the tree, at the wet black bark,
at the bright green leaves blowing in the wind.

Eric appeared earlier. He waved as he passed through the
sitting room and I waved back. He didn't say anything. His
smile looked a little distant. Perhaps he's fallen out with me,
or he wants to be left alone for some reason. When he passes
through the sitting room and doesn't say anything I decide that
I'm not going to go to the dining room for the evening meal.
Perhaps then he'll feel bad about things.

I get up out of my chair and go back to my room. The
nurses use the wheelchair because they don't have the time to
amble along the long corridor at breakfast, lunch and dinner.
When I'm in my room I lie on my bed and look at the little
rectangular window until it's dark outside. I haven't turned
on the light. A red LED in the fire alarm on the ceiling, and
a green LED in the emergency light above the door, each cast
their shadows on the walls and floor.

The doctor doesn't think that my manuscript is quite ready
for publication. I suppose it's his way of saying that he doesn't
like what I've written, or that he thinks it exceptionally ter-

rible. He proposed that I consider starting again, at the beginning – another beginning; perhaps a novel set during the second world war. He told me about something he'd read, a true story of a man living in a lighthouse during the German occupation of Belgium, a young woman murdered in mysterious circumstances.

You would expect me to write in detail about my treatment, with a certain black fascination perhaps: the neon blue colour of the cytotoxic, anti-neoplastic drugs delivered intravenously; the x-ray machine orbiting my body; the ionizing radiation beams invisibly penetrating my flesh; the lingering destruction of bone marrow, hair follicles and the digestive tract.

But most of my time is spent sitting in various waiting rooms that all look more or less the same, and when the doctors finally come to explaining the progression of things to me I'm always too exhausted to listen. Each time I visit the hospital I leave feeling worse than previously. I barely remember being pushed back to my room, too weak to walk.

During the short days of recuperation, I am wheeled to the sitting room and left in my wheelchair by the window so that the nurses can change my bed linen at their leisure. Sometimes a volunteer comes to read to me from the doctor's second world war book, but she isn't very educated, and in addition to her struggling with the pronunciation of certain words, she repeatedly stops in the middle of a sentence to ask me why I want to hear about such awful things. I look at her as she reads, at her name written on a badge pinned to her apron above her left breast, her voice drifting in and out of hearing.

Whenever she looks at me, I turn away to face the window, embarrassed by my hairless, disfigured scalp. The tree's branches move against the sky, each thinning cluster of young leaves settling to stillness, before the wind again rises to disturb their peace.

'The remaining survivors walked for days from village to village in the unbearable cold of winter. The houses had been destroyed and the pigs had been slaughtered and left to rot in the yards. One of the men had eaten meat from a putrefying carcass and had been too weak to survive diarrhoea. Now the remains of the slaughtered animals were frozen and buried beneath a metre of snow. In one village they found an old woman, the only inhabitant remaining, though most of the houses had been left relatively undamaged. Human limbs were hanging to cure in her larder: a handless arm tied through the wrist, and the upper halves of two legs. For a while they couldn't understand what they were looking at. The old woman stood in a corner of the parlour, her hands fidgeting nervously with the buttons of her coat. She'd found the dead soldier in the woods, she said.'

46

O N T H E 2 7 T H of June I'm told that I have a visitor – a colleague from Siemens. For a few moments, as I'm wheeled in to meet him, I can't remember his name. We shake hands and wait for the nurse to leave the visiting room. I look at his face and smile a little. He has short brown hair and the vague traces of teenage acne beneath two prominent cheekbones.

I'm relieved when I remember that his name is Maurice. I don't know his surname. I doubt whether I ever knew his surname. We were never what you might have called 'friends'. I find it a little strange that he's decided to come and visit me.

I smile again and ask how he is, before adding that it's nice to see him after all this time. He nods his head and stutters, his mobile phone clenched in his hand. He seems a little shocked by my appearance. I try to think of something to say, but it's impossible. We sit in silence.

'I just thought I'd come to see you,' he says after what seems like a long time. 'I heard on Facebook that you were in hospital, but I didn't know that it was . . .' He looks at the floor, his eyes searching the carpet. 'I didn't know that it was . . .'

'A psychiatric hospital?'

'Yes.'

'I have cancer and I'm insane,' I say. 'Life's a bitch.'

I shrug my shoulders. You're expected to say such things

when you have cancer, perhaps if only to put your perfectly healthy friends and family at ease in your presence. But it's the first time that I've found myself uttering such a ridiculous sentence.

'There isn't much to say on the subject,' I say. 'I mean on the subject of cancer. I smoked three packets of cigarettes a day for twenty years.'

I turn my wheelchair and look out of the large window at the smooth, polished façade of a concrete wall. A small tree the size of a newly planted sapling grows in front of the wall, its foliage almost perfectly symmetrical.

'This view reminds me of Mies van der Rohe's Barcelona pavilion. It's strange how many modernist homes resemble psychiatric hospitals.'

I look at Maurice, pleased with my clever remark. He turns to look out of the window. 'Actually, I came here to ask you something. I was wondering if you'd like to work for me? I've started my own company.'

'Work for you?'

'I mean when you're better. When you're living in your own place.'

'I'm not sure if I would be able to cope, Maurice.'

'Think about it for a while. You can come and go as you please as long as you get the work done.'

'What's your company called?' I ask.

'Maurice Pieters. It isn't very original, I know. We were going to use the name of a fruit but they were all taken. I nearly decided on the name Pineapple until my wife pointed out that it contains the word "apple". So what do you think? Are you going to consider it?'

'Of course. Things are just difficult for me at the moment.'

'I understand, Raymond. You don't have to explain yourself to me.'

I nod my head and turn to look out of the window. After what might have been two or three minutes of silence, I hear Maurice shifting his position on the sofa.

'Anyway,' he says. 'I'd better be going.'

I turn my wheelchair and shake his hand as he stands up.

'I'm running the Brussels marathon for charity in a few months.' He stops and thinks about saying something else, then changes his mind and decides not to bother. I nod my head and wish him good luck. When he's left the nurse comes to push me back to the sitting room, where she helps me back into the chair by the window. In the late afternoon, the sun breaks through the clouds, momentarily lighting the garden. I watch the rose bushes swaying gently in the breeze, their heavy, pink flowers nodding peacefully above the sunlit grass. At five o'clock the nurse returns to give me my medication.

O N THURSDAY AFTERNOONS I attend the art therapy class. There is a new student sitting at a table by the door – an overweight woman with curly red hair, wearing a multi-coloured, elasticated blouse. The teacher welcomes the new student by introducing himself and by giving a short explanation of what art therapy is, what it aims to achieve.

'You must be Hilary?'

The overweight woman nods. I look at the back of her head, at her curly red hair.

'Thank you for joining us, Hilary. My name's Richard. I am an artist first and foremost. I make paintings in oil and watercolour, and commissioned works of sculpture in bronze and iron. I have a degree in fine art and a masters degree in art therapy, and I am registered with the Belgian Association of Art Therapists.'

He flicks his black fringe from his forehead and brushes his fingers through his hair.

'So what is Art Therapy? Well, let's see. As children, we loved to paint pictures. Everyone remembers painting a picture at school and taking it home to show to their parents. Well, when we painted those pictures as children, it wasn't so much the getting a house to look like a house that was important, but it was the emotions that were important. We wanted to communicate feelings: how we felt when we played in the garden with our friends, or when we took our dog for a walk in the park. And so this is what is important to us today, here, in this class: we want to paint how something makes us feel. An ability to paint, to make something look like something, is not important.'

I pick up a pencil and start to draw one of the chairs, the window and its view of a metal fence.

'Raymond, please wait. It would be polite to wait. We have a new student.'

The fat redhead looks over her shoulder at me. I put my pencil down. As the teacher continues with his introduction, I look at each of the students in the class. They have interesting faces only because they belong to patients in a psychiatric hospital. If I were an artist attempting to paint one of the other students, I would have to call the painting 'Psychiatric Patient' to imbue the image with meaning. Perhaps I could do a series of numbered paintings and title them 'Psychiatric Patient #1', 'Psychiatric Patient #2', etc.

Of course I never learned to paint human beings at the École Nationale Supérieure des Arts Décoratifs. I was only ever taught to draw objects and to colour them in like a child: a table, a chair, a microwave oven; the effects of light on metal, plastic and glass. A human eye placed on a dissecting table would be a distinct possibility; but two human eyes gazing half hidden from behind the seemingly impenetrable mask of an expressive face . . . No, it isn't possible for me. Besides, painting is a skill to be acquired like any other over a certain period of time, and most paintings are as artless as a drawing for a design brief.

'As always, there are some books at the front to help you if you're struggling to inspire yourself, but I would really love for you to paint whatever you want, whether something from your past, or something from your future. Whether it's something real, something at home that has happened to you personally, or something entirely fictitious from inside your own head. It is entirely up to you as an artist.'

I pick up my pencil and continue to draw the chair: the rounded plastic seat, the hole in the backrest, the thin, metal legs.

The teacher circles slowly around the room offering advice and encouragement. He stops and looks at my drawing.

'I like what you're doing, Raymond. Why don't you sketch in the rosebushes?'

I look out of the window at the roses.

'I don't know how to draw living things.'

'It's never too late to learn, Raymond.'

I look back at the chair.

'I've been offered a job when I get out of the hospital. I probably need to practise drawing inanimate objects.'

48

I'VE BEEN GIVEN an apartment in Veurne, its interior furnished by a local charity dedicated to such purposes: a television, a sofa, a bed, a wardrobe, a cooker and a refrigerator, a personal computer and a games console. Even one or two books neatly placed on an otherwise empty shelf.

All of the residents are in a similar position to myself, and so the building is quiet and peaceful. Occasionally I will hear a door opening and closing, rubber-soled shoes on the polished linoleum.

A sixty-year-old homosexual lives in the apartment next door. He has a budgerigar which occasionally sings for an hour in the afternoon when the sun is shining. At night, when the budgerigar is asleep in its cage, the homosexual complains to himself and cries.

I sit at the table and look out of the window. There are five small trees and a rectangle of grass. Opposite my building, there is another building. It could be a reflection in a three-storey mirror, except that sometimes a man who is slightly older than myself is sitting at the window where I would be sitting.

I have spent my days here talking to my friends on THAILOVELINKS.COM. Pamela asked when I'm going to go to Thailand to meet her. I thought about telling her the news of my prognosis, but in the end I didn't bother. I suppose it doesn't seem to be very important.

Occasionally I find myself staring out of the window with a longing for life that I have never once felt before. The rectangle of sky above the building opposite has been blue and cloudless for weeks. The sun appears in the left hand corner of the window at three o'clock in the afternoon. I sit and stare until it falls behind the buildings to the right hand corner of the window, the interior of my apartment bleached in a soft yellow light, the delineations of the walls and doors barely visible.

Last night I found myself walking to a massage parlour on Noordstraat, but I was worried the girls would be repelled by my body, and a feeling of shame grew heavier as I approached. I turned back, or rather I made a circumambulation of the city, sheepishly crossing the street and assuming a ridiculous air of having planned a destination as I wandered aimlessly away. Eventually I found myself in a little park with a square which reminded me of the Bruges square I'd dreamt about. I sat on a bench beneath the plane trees and the darkened façades of a dozen or so elegant townhouses, the nightmare circus and the dread of the roaming animals playing through my mind.

Recovering my strength as I enjoyed the quiet evening, I thought about my life and smoked a packet of cigarettes, but my presence on the bench had started to arouse the suspicion of an elderly woman in one of the townhouses opposite the park. She turned on a light in a downstairs room and stood at the window to make me aware that I was being watched. She probably thought I was a vagrant intending to sleep the night under one of the perennial bushes. The old crone came and went for three-quarters of an hour, disappearing through a door at the back of the room, reappearing holding a large telephone receiver to her ear. Sometimes she looked as though she was talking to someone in another room, tilting her head a little to raise her voice, I presumed to a half deaf husband who couldn't rouse himself to come and look. Eventually the

old woman's attention grew irritating and I'd regained enough
strength to make my way back to my apartment. I left the
park under her gaze and crossed the street towards her front
door. She'd turned off the light and was standing in the darkness, a vague shadow that stepped back from the glass as I
approached and knocked. I could hear her slippered little feet
scuttling away down the hall, a whisper of air as an interior
door was opened somewhere at the back of the house. After a
minute or two, a man's face appeared, watery blue eyes peering
over a pair of half-moon spectacles. I pushed the door open,
knocking the old man to the floor. He fell slowly, as though
the fall had been separated into distinct, unrelated parts: his
legs buckling as he collapsed sideways to his knees, his arms
splaying pathetically as he dropped forwards on to his hands,
his head finally colliding against the bottom of the stairs. I
would have laughed but his wife was screaming from the door
at the end of the hall. As I grabbed the old man by the collar
and dragged him across the floor, she fell backwards, clattering
into the door and grabbing her chest. I'd never seen anyone
have a heart attack before. She lay on her side, her lips turning
blue as her fingers twisted her knitted cardigan into knots. I
dragged the old man into the kitchen and looked through the
drawers for a knife. He was begging me to help his wife, to call
an ambulance, but nothing felt as though it was really happening. I shouted and cursed the old woman for the ridiculous
state of her kitchen cabinets. And she had the audacity to stand
at the window and stare at me like that.

As I left, I noticed a smear of blood on the wall and a blood-
stain on the carpet at the bottom of the stairs. I thought that
perhaps a grandchild had spilt paint or tomato sauce, wiping
his hands as he played. I closed the heavy front door quietly
behind me, my eyes glancing again at the old man cradling his
wife at the end of the hall.

The carpet was beautiful, too, a deep golden plush woven with a swirling pattern of flowers. Perhaps they could contract the services of a professional cleaning company in the morning when they'd recovered from being attacked.

49

M Y MOBILE PHONE has been ringing for most of the
morning. I was supposed to start working for Maurice
today. I've been sitting nervously at the window waiting for the
police to come and arrest me. Every time I hear a door opening
and closing somewhere in the corridor my heart pounds uncontrollably against my chest. I'm still not sure whether any of
those terrible things really happened. I don't want to think that
I am capable of attacking an old man and woman like that.

At two o'clock in the afternoon I heat a meal-for-one in the
microwave – chicken breast in a spicy herb sauce with rice.
I empty the carton on to a plate and eat at the table by the
window. The sauce is green and delicious and tastes of lime
and coriander.

When I've finished, I call Maurice. A receptionist answers
and I'm put on hold. I listen to a modern, vaguely sinister
slow dance track, and picture the foyer at the other end of
the line: white, grey, chrome, perhaps a splash of colour – an
orange cow's head mounted on the wall, an antique chandelier
sprayed pink. After ten seconds I hang up.

I smoked my last cigarette three hours ago and I need to go
to the tabac. The palms of my hands are beginning to sweat
and I have a headache.

I turn the computer on and log into the chatroom on
THAILOVELINKS.COM. Pamela has gone to stay with her

sister in Phuket and so I say hello to a girl called Dorothy. She doesn't reply and I look at the photos on her profile page. I find it easy to imagine myself licking her pussy and arsehole. She has a provocative stare and a mischievous smile. In one of the photographs she's sitting with her legs spread on the edge of a bed, her hands draped between her legs to obscure her bright pink panties. It looks as though the photograph was taken inside an expensive hotel room. There's a remote control on the bedside cabinet and a paper 'Do Not Disturb' sign that you hang over the door handle.

I say hello to her again and wait for her to respond. After twenty minutes I think about saying hello for the third time. I could ask her about her day. They seem to like to talk about things like that. What they did at work, what their colleagues said, how their boss is behaving with everyone.

I hear a door opening and closing in the entrance hall downstairs. I lean towards the window. There's a car in the car park that I haven't seen before. I sit back in my chair and listen, staring into space, listening.

When I look back at the screen, Dorothy has left the chatroom. I pick my computer monitor up off the table and throw it violently against the wall. The glass shatters and the plastic casing breaks into several pieces. I look at it for a moment, at the large circuit board attached by coloured wires to the various loose pieces of the broken monitor, my gaze slowly drifting across the carpet to a cigarette burn and a dark brown stain.

I listen for the sound of a door opening, slippers walking across the polished linoleum, lowered voices – anything to suggest that someone along the corridor is going downstairs to report me to the warden.

It's impossible to leave the building without walking past the warden's office. I'll have to wait until five o'clock before I can go to the tabac for a packet of cigarettes. The warden goes home at five o'clock. I sit back in the chair by the window and look at the trees, at the grass, at the man sitting at the window in the building opposite. He's looking at me, sitting sideways to the window like I am but in the opposite direction. We stare at one another. I look away, then glance back: he's looking away, too, his head tilted slightly towards the ground as though he's looking at the trees, watching their leaves blowing in the wind.

I stand up shaking my head and mumbling to myself as I pick up the computer's hard drive, screaming as I throw it violently against the wall. The rectangular box reduces itself to a pile of broken plastic and twisted metal. I stand over what remains of the computer, swaying backwards and forwards, my eyes half closing, closing, opening and closing. I don't move except to sway a little, backwards and forwards. I don't feel capable of moving, even when I hear the sound of the warden locking his office and the main door closing behind him as he makes his way towards the car park.

Hours pass; fatigue drains my body. It's getting late and the room has been lit by a soft white moonlight. I walk over to the sofa and lie down. A cluster of stars is visible through the window, pale blue flickerings above the roof of the building opposite.

50

FROM A DISTANCE the villa appears much as I left it, the dunes perhaps a little closer, higher than before, the perimeter wall almost buried.

I leave the road and struggle across the sand. My legs are aching and barely able to hold my weight, my feet blistered and burning. On the outskirts of Veurne I stole a car from a petrol station forecourt. The owner had left his keys on the roof as I was passing. If he hadn't been so careless, I wouldn't have been presented with the opportunity.

I set the car on fire in an empty car park, lighting some pieces of paper and clothing under one of the seats. The theft had exhilarated me, a moment's euphoria which soon wore off, replaced by fatigue and the more prosaic concerns of destroying the evidence.

I sit against a drift of sand in the warm early morning sunshine and look at the villa. I am only perhaps a mile away, but these last yards seem to stretch beyond the horizon. I rest my head and listen to the calls of the skylarks, the sound of the sea drowned by their strangely sinister alarms.

Joy had downloaded a beach recording to her mobile phone in an attempt to help her sleep. It played throughout the night from a pair of earphones, and she would wake every morning to the hushed waves of a gentle sea. But the recording was looped and the faded edit obvious. On the few occasions that I slept in her bed, the quiet hissing whispers of the waves would trouble me like tinnitus, each return to the beginning of the recording more wearying than the last.

We often think in terms of beginnings and ends. I've been trying to remember how the ghost writer chose to end his book. Wishing to soften the blow, perhaps he'd written a paragraph or two recalling Joy in full vigour. It seems a reasonable convention, to end at the beginning.

On my last day of life I will sit in the wicker chair watching the sea, the waves rolling gently on to the beach. Each wave like the last. Then nothing.

ACKNOWLEDGEMENTS

It has become something of a fashion to make what amounts to an awards ceremony acceptance speech at the end of a novel, and so I would like to make my own, if only for the reason that I may not have the opportunity to do so again.

Although I cannot find it within myself to say that *The Beginning of the End* would not have been written but for the help of any particular person, I would like to thank my girlfriend Katie Grogan for her almost saintly patience, our now dead cat Sally, and our dog Alfie – all constant friends, each offering their own encouragement.

At a time when the novel is in danger of becoming only a soporific balm, this book might not have been published but for Nicholas Royle at Salt. I would like to thank him for his taste, his editorial expertise and his enthusiasm.

ALSO AVAILABLE FROM SALT

ELIZABETH BAINES
Too Many Magpies (978-1-84471-721-7)
The Birth Machine (978-1-907773-02-0)

LESLEY GLAISTER
Little Egypt (978-1-907773-72-3)

ALISON MOORE
The Lighthouse (978-1-907773-17-4)
The Pre-War House and Other Stories (978-1-907773-50-1)
He Wants (978-1-907773-81-5)

ALICE THOMPSON
Justine (978-1-78463-031-7)
The Falconer (978-1-78463-009-6)
The Existential Detective (978-1-78463-011-9)
Burnt Island (978-1-907773-48-8)

MEIKE ZIERVOGEL
Magda (978-1-907773-40-2)
Clara's Daughter (978-1-907773-79-2)